Charles Egbert Craddock

The Bushwhackers and Other Stories

Charles Egbert Craddock

The Bushwhackers and Other Stories

ISBN/EAN: 9783744750479

Printed in Europe, USA, Canada, Australia, Japan

Cover: Foto ©Andreas Hilbeck / pixelio.de

More available books at **www.hansebooks.com**

THE
Bushwhackers
&
Other Stories

BY

Charles Egbert Craddock

AUTHOR OF "IN THE TENNESSEE MOUNTAINS," "THE
STORY OF OLD FORT LOUDON," ETC.

HERBERT S. STONE & COMPANY
CHICAGO & NEW YORK
MDCCCXCIX

COPYRIGHT 1899 BY
HERBERT S. STONE & CO.

THIRD IMPRESSION

CONTENTS

THE BUSHWHACKERS

THE BUSHWHACKERS

CHAPTER I

One might have imagined that there was some enchantment in the spot which drew hither daily the young mountaineer's steps. No visible lure it showed. No prosaic reasonable errand he seemed to have. But always at some hour between the early springtide sunrise and the late vernal sunset Hilary Knox climbed the craggy, almost inaccessible steeps to this rocky promontory, that jutted out in a single sharp peak, not only beetling far over the sea of foliage in the wooded valley below, but rising high above the dense forests of the slope of the mountain, from the summit of which it projected. Here he would stand, shading his eyes with his hand, and gaze far and near over the great landscape. At first he seemed breathless with eager expectation; then earnestly searching lest there should be aught overlooked; at last dully, wistfully dwelling on the scene in the full realization of the pangs of disappointment for the absence of something he fain would see.

Always he waited as long as he could, as if the chance of any moment might conjure into the landscape, brilliant with the vivid growths and tender grace of the spring, that for which he looked in vain. A wind would come up the gorge and flutter about him, as he stood poised on the upward slant of the rock, the loftiest point of the mountain. If it were a young and frisky zephyr, but lately loosed from the cave of Æolus, which surely

must be situated near at hand—on the
opposite spur perhaps, so windy was
the ravine, so tumultuous the contin-
ual coming and going of the currents
of the air,—he must needs risk his balance on the pinnacle of the crag to
hold on to his hat. And sometimes
the frolicsome breeze like other gay
young sprites would not have done
with playing tag, and when he thought
himself safe and lowered his hand to
shade his eyes, again the wind would
twitch it by the brim and scurry away
down the ravine, making all the trees
ripple with murmurous laughter as it
sped to the valley, while Hilary would
gasp and plunge forward and once
more clutch his hat, then again look
out to descry perchance what he so
ardently longed to see in the distance.
Some pleasant vision he surely must
have expected — something charming
to the senses or promissory of weal

or happiness it must have been; for his cheek flushed scarlet and his pulses beat fast at the very thought.

No one noticed his coming or going. All boys are a species of vagrant fowl, and with the daily migrations back and forth of a young mountaineer especially, no steady-minded, elder person would care to burden his observation. Another kind of fowl, an eagle, had built a nest in the bare branches at the summit of an isolated pine tree, of which only the lower boughs were foliaged, and this was higher even than the peak to which Hilary daily repaired for the earliest glimpse of his materialized hopes advancing down the gorge. The pair of birds only of all the denizens of the mountain took heed of his movements and displayed an anxiety and suspicion and a sort of fierce but fluttered indignation. It is impossible to say whether they were aware that their variety had grown rare in these parts, and that their capture, dead or alive, would be a matter of very considerable interest, and it is also futile to speculate as to whether they had any knowledge of the uses or range of the rifle which Hilary sometimes carried on his shoulder. Certain it is, however, the male bird muttered indignantly as he looked down at the young mountaineer, and was wont to agitatedly flop about the great clumsy nest of interwoven sticks where the female, the larger of the two, with a steady courage sat motionless, only her elongated neck and bright dilation of the eyes betokening her excitement and distress. The male bird was of a more reckless tendency, and often visibly strove with an intermittent intention of swooping down to attack the intruder, for Hilary was but a slender fellow of about sixteen years, although tall and fleet of foot. A good shot, too, he was, and he had steady nerves, despite the glitter of excitement in his eyes forever gazing down the gorge. Because of his absorption in this expectation he took no notice of the eagles, although to justify his long absences from home he often brought his rifle on the plea of hunting. How should he care to observe the birds when at any moment he might see the flutter of a guidon in the valley road, a mere path from this height, and hear the trumpet sing out sweet and clear in the silence of the wilderness! At any moment the wind might bring the sound of the tramp of cavalry, the clatter of the carbine and canteen, and the clanking of spur and saber as some wild band of guerrillas came raiding through the country.

For despite the solemn stillness that brooded in the similitude of the deepest peace upon the scene, war was still rife in the land. The theater of action was far from this sequestered region, but there had been times when the piny gorges were full of the more prickly growth of bayonets. The echoing crags were taught the thrilling eloquence of the bugle, and the mountains reverberated with the oratory of the cannon—for the artillery learned to climb the deer-paths. There was a fine panorama once in the twilight when a battery on the heights shelled the woods in the valley, and tiny white clouds with hearts of darting fire described swift aerial curves, the fuses burning brightly against the bland blue sky, ere that supreme moment of explosion when the bursting fragments hurtled wildly through the air.

Occasionally a cluster of white tents would spring up like mushrooms at the base of a mountain spur—gone as suddenly as they had come, leaving a bed of embers where the camp-fires had been, a vague wreath of smoke and little trace besides, for the felled trees cut for fuel made scant impression upon the densities of the wilderness, and the rocks were immutable.

And then for months a primeval silence and loneliness might enfold the mountains.

"Ef they kem agin, ef ever they kem agin, I'll jine 'em—I'll jine 'em," cried Hilary out of a full heart as he stood and gazed.

And this was the reason he watched daily and sometimes deep into the night, lest coming under cover of the darkness they might depart before the dawn, leaving only the embers of their camp-fires to tell of their vanished presence.

The prospect stirred the boy's heart. He longed to be in the midst of action,

to take a man's part in the great struggle, to live the life and do the faithful
devoir of a soldier. He was young
but he was strong, and he felt that here
he was biding at home as if he were
no more fit for the military duty he
yearned to assume than was the miller's daughter, Delia Noakes.

"I tole Dely yesterday ez I'd git her
ter l'arn me ter spin ef ye kep' me
hyar much longer," he said one day
petulantly to his mother. "I'll jes'
set an' spin like a sure-enough gal ef
ye won't let me go an' jine the army
like a boy."

"I ain't never gin my word agin yer
goin'," the widow would temporize,
alarmed by the possibility of his running away without permission if definitely forbidden to enlist, and therefore
craftily holding out the prospect of
her consent, which she knew he valued,
for he had always been a dutiful son.

"I hev never gin my word agin it—not sence ye hev got some growth—ye shot up as suddint ez Jonah's gourd in a single night. But I don't want ye ter jine no stray bands—ez mought be bushwhackers an' sech. Jes' wait till we git the word whar Cap'n Baker's command be—fur I want ye ter be under some ez kem from our deestric'—I'd feel so much safer bout'n ye, an' ye would be pleased, too, Cap'n Baker bein' a powerful fighter an' brave an' respected by all. Ye mus' wait, too, till I kin finish yer new shuts, an' knittin' them socks; I wouldn't feel right fur ye to go destitute—a plumb beggar fur clothes."

Hilary had never heard of Penelope's web, and the crafty device of raveling out at night the work achieved in the day, but to his impatience it seemed that his departure was indefinitely postponed for his simple outfit progressed no whit day by day, although his mother's show of industry was great.

The earth also seemed to have swallowed Captain Baker and his command; although Hilary rode again and again to the postoffice at a little mountain hamlet some ten miles distant, and talked to all informed and discerning persons whom the hope of learning the latest details of the events of the war had drawn thither, and could hear news of any description to suit the taste of the narrator—all the most reliable items of the "grape-vine telegraph," as mere rumor used to be called in those days—not one word came of Captain Baker.

His mother sometimes could control his outbursts of impatience on these occasions by ridicule.

"'Member the time, Hil'ry," she would say, glancing at him with waggish mock gravity in her eyes as they gleamed over her spectacles, "when ye offered ter enlist with Cap'n Baker's infantry year afore las', when the war fust broke out—ye warn't no higher than that biscuit block then—he tole ye that ye warn't up ter age or size or weight or height, an' ye tole him that thar war a plenty of ye ter pull a trigger, an' he bust out laughin' an' lowed ez he warn't allowed ter enlist men under fourteen. He said he thunk it war a folly in the rule, fur he had seen some mighty old men under fourteen —though none so aged ez you-uns. My, how he did laugh."

"I wish ye would quit tellin' that old tale," said her son, sulkily, his face reddening with the mingled recollection of his own absurdity and the seriousness with which in his simplicity he had listened to the officer's ridicule.

"An' ye war so special small-sized

and spindlin' then,'' exclaimed his mother, pausing in her knitting to take off her spectacles to wipe away the tears of laughter that had gathered at the recollection.

"I ain't small-sized an' spindling now,'' said Hilary, drawing himself up to his full height and bridling with offended dignity in the consciousness of his inches and his muscles. "I know ez Cap'n Baker or enny other officer would 'list me now, for though I ain't quite sixteen I be powerful well growed fur my age.''

As he realized this anew his flush deepened as he stood and looked down at the fire, while his mother covertly watched his expression. He felt it a burning shame that he should still linger here laggard when all his instinct was to help and sustain the cause of his countrymen. His loyalty was to the sense of home. His impulse was to repel the invader, although the majority of the mountaineers of East Tennessee were for the Union, and many fought for the old flag against their neighbors and often against their close kindred, so stanch was their loyalty in those times that tried men's souls.

One day, as Hilary, straining his eyes, stood on his perch on the crag, he beheld fluttering far, far away—was it a wreath of mist floating along the level, sinuous curves of the distant valley road—a wreath of mist astir on some gentle current of the atmosphere? He had a sudden sense of color. Did the vapor catch a prismatic glister from the sun's rays? And now faint, far, like the ethereal tones of an elfin horn, a mellow vibration sounded on the air. Hardly louder it was than the booming of a bee in the heart of a flower, scarcely more definite than the melody one hears in a dream, which one can remember, yet cannot recognize or sing again; nevertheless his heart bounded at the vague and vagrant strain, and he knew the fluttering prismatic bits of color to be the guidons of a squadron of cavalry. His heart kept pace with the hoofbeats of the horses. The lessening distance magnified them to his vision till he could discern now a bright glint of steely light as the sun struck on the burnished arms of the riders, and could distinguish the tints of the steeds—gray, blood-bay, black and roan-red; he could soon hear, too, the jingle of the spurs, the clank of sabers and carbines, and now and again the voices of the men, bluff, merry, hearty, as they rode at their ease. He would not lose sight of them till they had paused to pitch their camp at the foot of a great spur of the mountain opposite. There was a famous spring of clear, cold water there, he remembered.

The great spread of mountain ranges had grown purple in the sunset, with the green cup-like coves between filled to the brim with the red vintage of the afternoon light, still limpid, translucent, with no suggestion of the dregs of shadow or sediment of darkness in this radiant nectar. Nor was there token of coming night in the sky—all amber and pearl—the fairest hour of the day. No premonition of approaching sorrow or defeat, of death or rue, was in the gay bivouac at the foot of the mountain. The very horses picketed along the bank of the stream whickered aloud in obvious content with their journey's end, their supper, their drink, and their bed; the sound of song and jollity, the halloo, the loud, cheery talk of the troopers, rose as lightly on the air as the long streamers

of undulating blazes from the camp-
fires and the curling tendrils of the
ascending smoke. More distant groups
betokened the precaution of videttes at
an outpost. A sentinel near the road,
for the camp guard was posted betimes, was the only silent and grave
man in the gay company, it seemed
to Hilary, as he watched the gallant,
soldierly figure with his martial tread
marching to and fro in this solitary
place, as if for all the world to see.
For Hilary had made his way down the
mountain and was now on the outskirts
of the camp, the goal of all his military
aspirations.

He had come so near that a
sudden voice rang out on the evening air, and he paused as the sentry
challenged his approach. The rocky
river bank vibrated with the echo
of the soldier's imperative tones.

Hilary remembered that moment

always. It meant so much to him. Every detail of the scene was painted on his memory years and years afterward as if but yesterday it was aglow— the evening air that was so still, so filled with mellow, illuminated color, so imbued with peace and fragrance and soft content, such as one could imagine may pervade the realms of Paradise, was yet the vehicle for the limning of this warlike picture. The great purple mountains loomed high around; through the green valley now crept a dun-tinted shadow more like a deepening of the rich verdant color of the foliage than a visible transition toward the glooms of the night; the stream was steel-gray and full of the white flickers of foam; further up the water reflected a flare of camp-fires, broadly aglow, with great sprangles of fluctuating flame and smoke setting the blue dusk a-quiver with alternations of light and shade; there were the dim rows of horses, some still sturdily champing their provender, others dully drowsing, and one nearer at hand, a noble charger, standing with uplifted neck and thin, expanded nostrils and full lustrous eyes, gazing over the winding way, the vacant road by which they had come. Beyond were the figures of the soldiers; a few, who had already finished their supper, were rolled in their blankets with their feet to the fire in a circle like the spokes of a wheel to the hub. There, pillowed on their saddles, would they sleep all night under the pulsating white stars, for these swift raids were unencumbered with baggage, and the pitching of a tent meant a longer stay than the bivouac of a single night. Others were still at their supper, broiling rashers of bacon on the coals, or toasting a bird or chicken, split and poised on a pointed cedar stick before the flames. Socially disposed groups were laughing and talking beside the flaring brands, the firelight gleaming in their eyes, half shaded by the wide, drooping brims of their broad hats, and flashing on their white teeth as they rehearsed the incidents of the day or made merry with old scores. Now and then a stave of song would rise sonorously into the air as a big bass voice trolled out a popular melody—it was the first time Hilary had ever heard the sentimental, melancholy measures of "The Sun's Low Down the Sky, Lorena." Sometimes, by way of symphony, a tentative staccato variation of the theme would issue from the strings of a violin, borrowed from a neighboring dwelling, which a young trooper, seated leaning against the bole of a great tree, was playing with a deft, assured touch.

Hilary often saw such scenes afterward, but not even the reality was ever so vivid as the recollection of this fire-lit perspective glimmering behind the figure of the guard.

The two gazed at each other in the brief space of a second—the boy eager and expectant, the soldier's eyes dark, steady, challenging, under the broad, drooping brim of his soft hat. He was young, but he had a short-pointed dark beard, and a mustache, and although thin and lightly built, he was sinewy and alert, and in his long, spurred boots and gray uniform he looked sufficiently formidable with his carbine in his hand.

"Who comes there?" he sternly demanded.

"A friend," quavered Hilary, and he could have utterly repudiated himself that his voice should show this tremor of excitement since it might seem to be that of fear in the estimation of this man, who defied dangers and knew no faltering, and had fought to the last moment on the losing side on many a stricken field, and was content to believe that duty and courage were as valid a guerdon in themselves as fickle victory, which perches as a bird might on the standard of chance.

"Advance, friend, and give the countersign," said the sentry.

It seemed to Hilary at the moment that it was some strange aberration of all the probabilities that he should not know this mystic word, this potent phrase, which should grant admission to the life of the camp that already seemed to him his native sphere. He advanced a step nearer, and while the sentinel bent his brow more intently upon him and looked firmly and negatively expectant, he gave in lieu of the watchword a full detail of his errand, —that he wished to be a soldier and fight for his country, and especially enlist with this squadron, albeit he did not know a single man of the command, nor even the leader's rank or name.

Hilary could not altogether account for a sudden change in the sentinel's face and manner. He had been very sure that he was about to be denied all admission according to the strict orders to permit no stranger within the lines of the encampment. The soldier stared at the boy a moment longer, then called lustily aloud for the corporal of the guard. For these were the days of the close conscription, when it was popularly said that the army robbed both the cradle and the grave for its recruits, so young and so old were the men accounted liable for military duty. The sentinel could but discern at a glance that Hilary was younger even than the limit for these later conscriptions, and that only as a voluntary sacrifice to patriotism were his services attainable. The corporal of the guard came forthwith—tall, heavy, broad-visaged, downright in manner, and of a blunt style of speech. But on his face, too, the expression of formidable negation gave way at once to a brisk alacrity of welcome, and he immediately conducted Hilary to another officer, who brought him to a little knoll where the captain commanding the squadron was seated by a brisk fire, half reclining on his saddle thrown on the ground. He was beguiling his leisure, and perhaps reinforcing a certain down-hearted tendency to nostalgia, by reading the latest letters he had from home—letters a matter of six months old now, and already read into tatters, but so illuminated between the lines with familiar pictures and treasured household memories that they were still replete with an interest that would last longer than the paper. Two or three other officers were playing cards by the light of the fire, and one, elderly and grave, was reading a book through spectacles of sedate aspect.

The measure of Hilary's satisfaction was full to the brim. Captain Baker, as he informed his mother when a little later he burst into the home-circle wild with delight in his adventure and his news, couldn't hold a candle to Captain Bertley. And rejoiced was he to be going at last and going with this officer. Hilary declared again and again that he wouldn't be willing to fight in any other command. He was going at last, and going with the only captain in all the world for him—the first and foremost of men! And yet only this morning he had not known that this paragon existed.

He was so a-quiver with excitement

and joy and expectation and pride that his mother, pale and tremulous as she made up his little bundle of long-delayed clothes, was a trifle surprised to hear him protest that he could not leave without bidding farewell to the Noakes family, who lived at the Notch in the mountain, and especially his old crony, Delia; yet Captain Bertley's trumpets would sound "boots and saddles" at the earliest glint of dawn. Delia was near his own age, and he had always magnanimously pitied her for not being a boy. Formerly she had meekly acquiesced in her inferiority, mental and physical, especially in the matter of running, although she made pretty fair speed, and in throwing stones, which she never could be taught to do with accurate aim. But of late years she had not seemed to "sense" this inferiority, so to speak, and once in reference to the war she had declared that she was glad to be a girl, and thus debarred from fighting, "fur killing folks, no matter fur whut or how, always seemed to be sinful!" When argued with on this basis she fell back on the broad and uncontrovertible proposition that "anyhow bloodshed war powerful onpleasant."

To see these friends once again Hilary had no time to waste. As he made his way along the sandy road with the stars palpitating whitely in the sky above the heavy forest, which rose so high on either hand as to seem almost to touch them, this deep, narrow passage looked when the perspective held a straight line to rising ground, ending in the sidereal coruscations, like the veritable way to the stars, sought by every ambitious wight since the days of the Cæsars. Hilary had never heard an allusion to that royal road, but as he walked along with a buoyant, steady step, his hat in his hand that the breeze might cool his hot brow and blow backward his long masses of fair hair, he followed indeed an upward path in the sentiments that quickened his pulses, for he was resolved upon duty and thinking high thoughts that should materialize in fine deeds. He was to do and dare! He would be useful and faithful and brave—brave! He had a reverence for the quality of courage—not for the sake of its emulous display, but for the spirit of all nobly valiant deeds. He had rejoiced in the very expression of the captain's eyes—so true and tried! He, too, would meet the coming years fairly. The raw recruit could see his way to the stars at the end of that mountain vista.

But it seemed a poor preparation for all this when he awoke the inmates of the Noakes cabin, for it was past midnight, with the news that he had ''jined the cavalry" and was to march at peep of dawn with Bertley's squadron. It is true that the elders crowded around him half dressed only, so hastily had they been roused, and expressed surprise, congratulations, and regrets in one inconsistent breath, and old Mrs. Dite, Delia's grandmother, bestowed on him a woolen comforter which she had knitted for him, and for which, improvidently, it being now near summer, he cared less than for the turmoil of excitement and interest they had manifested in his preferment, for he felt every inch a man and a soldier, and they respectfully seemed to defer to his new pretensions. Delia, however, the most unaccountable of girls—and girls are always unaccountable—put her arm over her eyes as she stood beside the mantelpiece, beneath which the embers had been stirred into a blaze for light, and turned her face to the wall and burst into tears. She wept with so much vehemence that her long plait of black hair hanging down her back swayed from side to side of her shoulders as she shook her head to and fro in the extremity of her woe. When the elders remonstrated with her, and declared this was no occasion for sorrow, she only lifted her tear-stained face for a moment to say in justification that she believed that bullets were too small to be dodged with any success when they were flying round promiscuously. And in the midst of the volley of laughter which this evoked from the old people, Hilary's voice rang out indignantly, "An' I ain't no hand ter dodge bullets, nuther."

"That's jes' what I am a-crying about," replied Delia, to the mischievous delight of the elders.

Thus the farewell to his old friends was not very exhilarating to Hilary.

Delia did not even at the last **unveil** her face or change her attitude against the wall. To shake hands he was obliged to pull her hand from her eyes by way of over her head, and in this maneuver he was moved to notice how much taller he had lately grown. Her hand was very limp and cold and wet with her tears—so wet that he had to wipe these tears from his own hand on the brim of his hat on his homeward way.

And when, as in sudden enchantment, darkness became light and night developed into dawn, when color renewed the landscape, and the dull sky grew red as if flushed with sudden triumph, and the black mountains turned royally purple in the distance and tenderly green nearer at hand, and the waters of the river leaped and flashed like a live thing, as with an actual joy in existence, and the great fiery sun, full of vital yellow flame, flared up over the eastern horizon, the squadron, with jingling spurs and clanking sabers, with carbines and canteens rattling, with the trumpet now and again sending forth those elated, joyous martial strains, so sweet and yet so proud, rode forth into a new day, and Hilary Knox, among the troopers and gallantly mounted, rode forth into a new life.

The bivouac fires glowed for a while, then fell to smoldering and died, leaving but a gray ash to tell of their presence here. Day by day the eagles in the great bare pine tree on the high rock at the summit of the mountain looked for Hilary to visit his point of observation and stir their hearts with fear and wrath. Time and again the male bird might have been seen to circle about at the usual hour for the boy's coming; first with apprehension lest his absence was too good to be true, then, with the courage of immunity undisciplined by fear, screaming and flouncing as if to challenge this apparition of quondam terror. Now and then the pair seemed to argue and collogue together upon the mystery of his non-appearance, and to chuffily compare notes, and seek to classify their impressions of this singular specimen of the animal kingdom. Perhaps, tabulated, their conclusions might stand thus: Genus, boy; habits, noisy; diet, omnivorous; element, mischief; uses, undiscovered and undiscoverable.

Long, long after the eagles had forgotten the intruder, after their brood, the two ill-feathered nestlings, had taken strongly to wing, after their nest, a mass of loose, but well collocated sticks and grass, had given way to the beat of the rain and the blasts of the wind, did Hilary's mother wearily gaze from the heights where the mountain cabin was perched down upon the curves of the valley road along which she had seen him riding away with that glittering train, and sigh and let her knitting fall from her nerveless hands, and wonder what would the manner of his home-coming be, or whether the future held at all a home-coming for him.

And her many sighs kept her heart sick and turned her hair very white.

CHAPTER II

It was a wonderful period of mental development for this wild young creature of the woods, when Hilary received in his sudden transition to the "valley kentry" his first adequate impressions of civilization. He learned that the world is wide; he beheld the triumphs of military science; he acquiesced in the fixed distinctions of rank, since he must needs concede the finer grades of capacity. But courage, the inherent, inimitable endowment, he recognized as the soul of heroism, and in all the arrogance of elation he became conscious that he possessed it. This it was that opened his stolid mind to the allurements of ambition. He rejoiced in an aspiration.

He was brave. That was his identity—his essential vitality! Was he ignorant, poor, the butt of the camp-fire jokes, because of his simplicity in the wide world's ways, slothful, slow, wild, and turbulent? He took heed of none of this! He was the bravest of the brave—and all the command knew it!

With an exultant heart he realized that Captain Bertley was aware of the fact, and often took account of it in laying his plans. The regiment of which this squadron was a part belonged to one of those brigades of light cavalry whose utility was chiefly in quick movements, in harassing an enemy's march, in following up and hanging on his retreat, and sometimes in making swift forced marches, appearing unexpectedly in distant localities far from the main body and adding the element of surprise to a sudden and furious onslaught. Often Hilary was among a few picked men sent out to reconnoiter, or as the rear-guard when the little band was retreating before a superior force and it was necessary to fight and flee alternately. It was now and again in these skirmishes that he had the opportunity to show his pluck and his strength and his cool head and his ready hand. More than once he had been the bearer of dispatches of great importance sent by him alone, disguised in citizen's dress and his destination a long way off. Thus did the captain commanding the squadron demonstrate his confidence in the boy's fidelity and courage and resource. For his ready wit in an emergency was hardly less than his courage.

"What did you do, then, with the Colonel's letter that you were to deliver at brigade head-quarters?"

asked the Captain in much agitation, but with a voice like thunder and a flashing eye, when one day Hilary returned from a fruitless expedition, with his finger in his mouth, so to speak, and a tale of having encountered Federal scouts, who had stopped and questioned him, and finally after suspiciously searching him, had turned him loose, believing him nothing more than he seemed—a peaceful, ignorant country boy.

Hilary glanced ruefully down at the hat that he swung in his hand, then with anxious deprecation at the Captain, whose face as he stood beside his horse, ready to mount, had flushed deeply red, either because of the reflection of the sunset clouds massed in the west or because of the recollection that he had earnestly recommended the boy to his superior officer, for this dangerous mission, and thus felt peculiarly responsible; for the letter had contained details relating to the Colonel's orders from brigade headquarters, his numbers, and other matters, the knowledge of which in the enemy's hands might precipitate his capture, together with all the detach-ment.

"It's gone, sir," mumbled Hilary, the picture of despair; "I never knowed what ter do, so—"

"So you let them have that letter—when I had told you how important it was!"

"I don't see how it could have been helped, since the boy was searched," said Captain Blake, the junior captain of the squadron, who was standing by. "I am glad he came back to let us know."

"That's why I done what I done," eagerly explained Hilary. "I—I—eat it."

"All of it?" cried Captain Bertley, with a flash of relief.

"Yes, sir, I swallowed it all bodaciously—just ez soon ez I seen 'em a-kemin' dustin' along the road."

"Well done, Baby Bunting!" cried the senior officer, for thus was Hilary distinguished among the troopers on account of his tender years.

The gruff Captain Blake laughed delightedly, a hoarse, discordant demonstration, much like the chuckling of a rusty old crow. He seemed to think it a good joke, and Hilary knew that he, too, was vastly relieved to have saved from the enemy such important information.

"Pretty bitter pill, eh?"

"Naw, sir," said Hilary, his eyes twinkling as he swung his hat in his hand, for he could never be truly military out of his uniform; "it war like eatin' a yard medjure of mustard plaster, bein' stiff ter swaller an' somehow goin' agin the grain."

The senior captain gravely commended his presence of mind, and said he would remember this and his many other good services. As he dismissed the young trooper and still standing, holding a sheet of paper against his saddle, began to write a report of the fate of the letter that had so threatened the capture of the whole command, Hilary overheard Captain Blake say in his bluff, extravagant way, "That boy ought to be promoted."

"What?" said Captain Bertley, glancing back over his shoulder with the pencil in his hand. "Baby Bunting with a command!"

Despite the ridicule of the idea Hilary's heart swelled within him as he strolled away, for he cared only to deserve the promotion and the confidence shown him, even if on account of his extreme youth and presumable irresponsibility he was debarred from receiving it.

He could not have said why he was not resentful of being called "Baby Bunting" by Captain Bertley. He felt it was in the nature of a courteous condescension that the officer should comment on the inadequacy of his age and the discrepancy between his limited powers and his valuable deeds—almost as a jesting token of affection, kindly meant and kindly received. But the name fell upon his ear often with a far different significance; the camp cry "Bye, oh, Baby Bunting," was intended to goad him to such a degree of anger as should make him the sport of the groups around the bivouac fire. The chief instigator of this effort was a big, brutal cavalryman, by name Jack Bixby. He had a long, red beard; long, reddish hair; small, twinkling, dark eyes, and a powerfully built, sinewy, well-compacted figure. He was superficially considered jolly and genial, for few of his careless companions were observant enough of moral phenomena or sufficiently students of human nature to take note of the fact that there was always a spice of ill-humor in his mirth. Malice or jealousy or grudging or a mean spirit of derision pervaded his merriment. He found great joy in ridiculing a raw country boy, whose lack of knowledge of the world's ways laid him liable to many mistakes and misconceptions, and at first Hilary's credulity in the big lies told him by Jack Bixby and his simplicity in acting upon them exposed him to the laughter of the whole troop. This was checked in one instance, however; having been instructed that it was an accepted detail of the observances of a soldier, Hilary was induced to advance with great ceremony one day, and duly saluting ask Captain Bertley how he found his health. The officer was standing on ground somewhat elevated above the site of the camp, in full gray uniform, a field-glass in his hand, his splendid charger at his shoulder, the reins thrown over his arm. The humble "Baby Bunting" approaching this august military object, and presuming to ask after the commanding officer's health, was in full view of a hundred or more startled and amazed veterans.

But Captain Bertley had seen and known much of this world and its ways. He instantly recognized the incident as a bit of malicious play upon the simplicity of the new recruit, and he took due note, too, of his own dignity. He realized how to balk the one and to support the other. He accepted the unusual and absurd demonstration concerning his health by saying simply that he was quite well, and then he kept the boy standing in conversation as to the state of a certain ford some distance up the river, with which Hilary was acquainted, having been of a scouting party which had been sent in that direction the previous day. The staring military spectators, their attention previously bespoken by Bixby, saw naught especial in the interview, the boy apparently having been summoned thither by order of the officer to make a report or give information, and thus the joke, attenuated to microscopic proportions, failed of effect. It had, however, very sufficient efficacy in recoil. Before dismissing Hilary the Captain asked how he had chanced to accost him in the manner with which he had approached him, and the boy in guilelessly detailing the circumstance, before he was admonished as to his credulous folly, betrayed Bixby as the perpetrator of the pleasantry at his expense, and what was far more serious at the expense of the officer. Jack Bixby, dull enough, as malicious people often are, or they would not otherwise let their malice appear—for they are not frank—did not see it in that light until he suddenly found himself under arrest and then required to mount the "wooden horse" for several weary hours.

"You'll be hung up by the thumbs next time, my rooster," said the sergeant, as he carried the sentence into effect. "The Cap'n ain't so mighty partial to your record, no hows. He asked me if you hadn't served with Whingan's rangers, ez be no better'n bushwhackers, an' ye know he is mighty partic'lar 'bout keepin' up the tone an' spirit o' the men."

THE BUSHWHACKERS

Hilary, contradictorily enough, lost all sense of injury and shame in sorrow that he should have divulged Bixby's agency in the matter and brought this disaster upon the trooper, who perhaps had only intended a little diversion, and had neither the good taste nor the good sense to perceive its offensiveness to the officer. Bixby *had* served in a band generally reputed bushwhackers, who did little more than plunder both sides, and in which discipline was necessarily slight. And thus after this episode they were better friends than before. True, in the days of dearth, for these men must needs starve as well as fight, when only rations of corn were served out, which the soldiers parched and ate by the fire, and which were so scanty that a strict watch was kept to prevent certain of them from robbing their own horses, on the condition and speed of which their very lives depended, Hilary, as in honor bound, being detailed for this duty, reported his greedy comrade, but in view of the half-famished condition of the troops Bixby's punishment was light, and the incident did not break off their outward semblance of friendship, although one may be sure Bixby kept account of it.

So the years went—those wild years of hard riding and hard fighting; sleeping on the ground under the open skies whether cloudy or clear—it was months after it was all over before Hilary could accustom himself to sleep in a bed; roused by the note of the trumpet, sometimes while the stars were yet white in the dark heavens, with no token of dawn save a great translucent, tremulous planet heralding the morn, and that wild, sweet, exultant strain of reveille, so romantic, so stirring, that it might seem as if it had floated down, proclaiming the day, from that splendid vanguard of the sun. So they went—those wild years, all at once over.

The end came on a hard-contested field, albeit only a thousand or so were engaged on either side. The squadron, in one of those wild reckless assaults of cavalry against artillery, for which the Confederate horse were famous in this campaign, had gone to the attack straight up a hill, while the muzzles of the big, black guns sent forth smoke and roar, scarcely less frightful than the bombs which were bursting among the horses and men riding directly at the battery. It was hard to hold the horses. Often they swerved and faltered, and sought to turn back. Each time Captain Bertley, with drawn sword, reformed the line, encouraging the men and urging them to the almost impossible task anew. At it they went once more, in face of shot and shell. Now and again Hilary, riding in the rear rank, with his saber at "the raise," heard a sharp, singing sibilance, which he knew was a minie-ball, whizzing close to his ear, and he realized that infantry was there a little to one side supporting the battery. The rush, the turmoil, the blare of the trumpets sounding "the charge," the clamor of galloping hoofs, of shouting men, the roar of cannon, the swift panorama of moving objects before the eye, the ever-quickening speed, and the tremendous sensation of flying through the air like a projectile—it was all like some wild tempest, some mad conflict of the elements. And suddenly Hilary became aware that he was flying through the air without any will of his own. The horse had taken the bit between his teeth, and maddened by the noise, the frenzy of the fight, was rushing on he knew not whither, his head stretched out, his eyes starting, straight up the hill unmindful of the trumpet now sounding the recall and the heavy pull of the boy on the curb. Hilary was far away in advance of the others when the line wheeled. A few more impetuous bounds and plunges, and he was carried in among the Federal guns, mechanically slashing at the gunners with his saber, until one of the men, with a well-directed blow, knocked him off his horse with the long, heavy sponge-staff. So it was that Hilary was captured. He surrendered to the man with the sponge-staff, for the others were busily limbering up the guns; they were to take position on a new site—one less exposed to attack and very commanding. They had more than they wanted in Hilary. He realized that as he was on his way to the rear under guard.   The engagement was practically at an end, and the successful Federals were keenly eager to pursue the retreating force and secure all the fruits of victory.   To be hampered with the disposition of prisoners at such a moment was hardly wise, when an active pursuit might cut off the whole command.   Therefore the few already taken, who were more or less wounded, were temporarily paroled in a neighboring hamlet, and Hilary, the war in effect concluded for him—for the parole was a pledge to remain within the lines and report at stated intervals to the party granting it—found himself looking out over a broad white turnpike in a flat country, down which a cloud of dust was all that could be seen of the body of cavalry so lately contending for every inch of ground.

Now and again a series of white

puffs of smoke from amidst the hill-
ocks on the west told that the battery
of the Federals was shelling the woods
which their enemy had succeeded in
gaining, the shells hurtling high above
the heads of their own infantry marching forward resolutely, secure in the
fact of being too close for damage.
Presently the battery became silent.
Their vanguard was getting within
range of their own guns, and a second
move was in order. The boy watched
the flying artillery scurrying across the
plain, as he struck down a "dirt-road"
which intersected the turnpike, and
soon he noticed the puffs of white
smoke from another coign of vantage
and the bursting of shells still further
away.

"Them dogs barkin' again! Waal,
I'm glad ter be wide o' thar mark,"
said a familiar voice at his elbow; the
speaker was Bixby, a paroled prisoner,

too, having been captured further down the hill during the general retreat.

Hilary was not ill-pleased to see him at first, especially as something presently happened which made him solicitous for the advice and guidance of an older head than his own. By one of the vicissitudes of war victory suddenly deserted the winning side, and presently here was the erstwhile successful party in full retreat, swarming over the flat country, the battery scurrying along the turnpike with two of its guns missing, captured as they barked with their mouths wide open, so to speak. The hurrying crash and noisy rout went past like the phantasmagoria of a dream, and these two prisoners were presently left quite outside the Federal lines by no act or volition of their own, and yet apparently far enough from Bertley's squadron, for the pursuit was not pressed, both parties having had for the nonce enough of each other. The first object of the two troopers was to procure food of which they stood sadly in need. They set forth to find the nearest farmhouse, Hilary on his own horse, which in the confusion had not been taken from him when he was disarmed, and Bixby easily caught and mounted a riderless steed that had been in the engagement, but was now cropping the wayside grass.

A thousand times that day Hilary wished, as they went on their journey together, that he had never seen this man again. All Jack Bixby's methods were false, and it revolted Hilary, educated to a simple but strict code of morals, to seem to share in his lies and his dubious devices to avoid giving a true account of themselves. In fact their progress was menaced with some danger. Having little to distinguish them as soldiers, for the gray cloth uniform in many instances had given place to the butternut jeans, the habitual garb of the poorer classes of the country, they could be mistaken for citizens, peacefully pursuing some rustic vocation, and this impression Bixby sought to impose on every party who questioned them. He feared to meet the Federals, because of their paroles, which showed them to be prisoners and yet out of the lines, and he thought this broken pledge might subject them to the penalty of being strung up by the neck.

"That air tale 'bout our bein' in the lines an' the lines shrinkin' till we got out o' 'em ain't goin' ter go down with no sech brash fellers," he argued with some reason, for the probabilities seemed against them.

And now he dreaded an encounter

with Union men, non-combatants, for the same reason. He slipped off his boot at one time and hid the paper under the sole of his foot. "Ef we-uns war ter be sarched they wouldn't look thar, mos' likely." And finally when they reached the house of an aged farmer, who with partisan cordiality welcomed and fed them, declaring that although he was too old to fight he could thus help on the southern cause, Bixby took advantage of his host's short absence from the dining-room to strike a match which he discovered in a candlestick on the mantel piece, for the season was too warm for fires, and lighting the candle he held the parole in the flame till the paper was reduced to a cinder; then he hastily extinguished the candle.

When once more on the road, however, Bixby regretted his decision. For aught he knew they were still within the Federal lines. The Union troops had doubtless been reinforced, for they were making a point of holding this region at all hazards. He was a fool he said to have burnt his parole—it was his protection. If he were taken now by troops not in the extreme activities of resisting a spirited cavalry attack, who had time to make his capture good, and means of transportation handy, he would be sent off to Camp Chase or some other prison, and shut up there till the crack of doom, whereas his parole rendered him for the time practically free.

"Why didn't you keep me from doin' it, Hil'ry?"

"Why, I baiged an' baiged an' besought ye 'fore we went in the house ter do nothin' ter the paper," said Hilary, wearied and excited and even alarmed by his companion's vacillations, so wild with fear had Bixby become. "I wunk at ye when the old man's back was turned. I even tried ter snatch the paper whenst ye put yer boot-toe on the aidge of a piece of it on the ha'thstone an' helt it down till it war bu'nt."

"I war a fool," said Bixby, gloomily. "I wish I hed it hyar now."

"I tole ye," said Hilary, for he had spent the day in urging the fair and open policy, let come what might of it, "I tole ye ez I war a-goin' ter show my parole ter the fust man ez halts me, an' ef I be out'n the lines, an' he won't believe my tale, let him take it out on me howsumdever the law o' sech doin's 'pears. Nobody could expec' me ter set an' starve on that hillside till sech time ez the Fed'rals throw out thar line agin."

"I wisht I hed my parole agin," said Bixby, more moodily still.

Down the road before them suddenly

they saw a dust, and a steely glitter—
not so strong a reflection, however, as
marching infantry throws out. A
squad of cavalry was approaching at a
steady pace. Jack Bixby's first idea
was flight; this the condition of the
jaded horse rendered impolitic. Then
he thought of concealment—in vain.
On either hand the level, plowed
fields afforded not the slightest bush as
a shield. The only thicket in sight
was alongside the road and now in line
with the approaching party whom it
so shadowed that it was impossible to
judge by uniform or accoutrements to
which army they belonged.

"Hil'ry," said Jack Bixby, "let's
stick ter the country-jake story; I'll
say that I be a farmer round hyar
somewhar, an' pretend that you air my
son. That'll go down with any party."

"I be goin' ter tell the truth myself, an' show my parole, whoever they

be; that's the right thing," said Hilary, stoutly.

"But I ain't got no parole," quavered Bixby.

"Tell the truth an' I'll bear ye out," said Hilary. "Tell 'em that thar be so many parties — Feds an' Confeds an' Union men an' bushwhackers, an' we-uns got by accident out'n the lines an' ye took alarm an' *dee*stroyed yer parole. I'll bear ye out an' take my oath on it; an' ye know the old man war remarkin' on them cinders on the aidge o' the mantel shelf an' ha'th-stone ez we left the house."

"Hil'ry," said Bixby, as with a sudden bright idea—anything but the truth seemed hopeful to him—"I'll tell ye. I'll take yer parole an' claim it ez mine, an' pretend that ye air my son—non-combatant, jes' a boy, ez ye air."

"But it's got *my* name on it. It's

a-parolin' of *me*," said Hilary, "an' I *ain't* no non-combatant."

"But I'll claim your name; I'll be Hil'ry Knox, an' tall ez ye air, yer face shows ye ain't nuthin' but a boy. Nobody wouldn't disbelieve it."

"I won't do it! I won't put off a lie on 'em! I hev fought an' fought an' I'll take the consekences o' what I done—all the consekences o' hevin' fought. *I* am Hilary Knox, an' I be plumb pledged by my word of honor. But I'll bear ye out in the fac's, an' thar's nuthin' ter doubt in the fac's— they air full reasonable."

He had taken the paper out of his ragged breast-pocket to have it in readiness to present to the advance guard, who had perceived them and had quickened the pace for the purpose of halting them. Perhaps Bixby had no intention, save, by sleight-of-hand, to possess himself of the paper.

Perhaps he thought that having it in his power the boy would hardly dare to contradict the story he had sketched and the name he intended to claim as the owner of the parole; if Hilary should protest he could say his son was weak-minded, an imbecile, a lunatic. He made a sudden lunge from the saddle and a more sudden snatch at the paper. But the boy's strong hand held it fast. Jack Bixby hardly noted the surprise, the indignation, the reproach in Hilary's face—almost an expression of grief—as he turned it toward him. With the determination that had seized him to possess the paper, Bixby struck the boy's wrist and knuckles a series of sharp, brutal blows with the back of a strong bowie-knife, which had been concealed in his boot-leg at the surrender. They palsied the clutch of the boy's left hand. But as the quivering fingers opened, Hilary caught the falling paper with his right hand.

"Let go, let go!" cried Jack Bixby in a frenzy; "else I'll let you hev the blade—there, then!—take the aidge—ez keen ez a razor!"

The steel descended again and again, and as the boy was half dragged out of the saddle the blood poured down upon the parole. It would have been hard to say then what name was there!

A sudden shout rang out from down the road. The approaching men had observed the altercation, and mending their pace, came on at a swift gallop.

With not a glance at them, Jack Bixby turned his horse short around and fled as fast as the animal could go, striking out of the road and into the woods as soon as he reached the timbered land.

Poor "Baby Bunting," dragged out of his saddle, fell down in the road

beneath his horse's hoofs, and all covered with white dust and red blood
there he lay very still till the cavalry-
men came up and found him.

For this was what they called him—
"*Poor Baby Bunting!*" They were a
small reconnoitering party of his own
comrades, and it was with a hearty
good will that they pursued Jack Bixby
who fled, as from his enemies, through
the brush. Perhaps his enemies would
have been gentler with him than his
quondam friends could they only have
laid hands on him, for they all loved
"Baby Bunting" for his brave spirit
and his little simplicities and his hearty
good-comradeship. Hilary recognized
none of them. He only had a vague
idea of Captain Bertley's face with a
grave anxiety and a deep pity upon it
as the officer gazed down at him when
he was borne past on the stretcher to
the field hospital where his right arm

was taken off by the surgeon. He was treated as kindly as possible, for the remembrance of his gallant spirit as well as humanity's sake, and when at last he was discharged from the more permanent hospital to which he had been removed he realized that he had indeed done with war and fine deeds of valiance, and he set out to return home, tramping the weary way to the mountain and his mother.

After that fateful day, when maimed and wan and woebegone he came forth from the hospital and journeyed out from among the camps and flags and big guns and all the armaments of war, thrice splendid to his backward gaze, it seemed to him that he had left there more than was visible—that noble identity of valor for which he had revered himself.

For he found as he went a strange quaking in his heart. It was an alien thing, and he strove to repudiate it, and ached with helpless despair. When he came into unfamiliar regions, and a sudden clatter upon the lonely country road would herald the approach of mounted strangers, halting him, the convulsive start of his maimed right arm with the instinct to seize his weapons and the sense of being defenseless utterly would so unnerve him that he would give a disjointed account of himself, with hang-dog look and faltering words. And more than once he was seized and roughly handled and dragged to headquarters to show his papers and be at last passed on by the authorities.

He began to say to himself that his courage was in his cavalry pistol.

"Before God!" he cried, "me an' my right arm an' my weepon air like saltpetre an' charcoal an' sulphur—no 'count apart. An' tergether they mean *gunpowder!*"

And doubly bereaved, he had come in sight of home.

But his mother fell upon his neck with joy, and the neighbors gathered to meet him. The splendors of the Indian summer were deepening upon the mountains, with gorgeous fantasies of color, with errant winds harping æolian numbers in the pines, with a translucent purple haze and a great red sun, and the hunter's moon, most luminous. The solemnity and peace stole in upon his heart, and revived within him that cherished sense of home, so potent with the mountaineer, and in some wise he was consoled.

Yet he hardly paused. In this lighter mood he went on to the settlement, eager that the news of his coming should not precede him.

There was the bridge to cross and the

rocky ascent, and at the summit stood the first log cabin of the scattered little hamlet. From the porch, overgrown with hop vines, he heard the whir of a spinning wheel. He saw the girl who stood beside it before she noticed the sound of his step. Then she turned, staring at him with startled recognition, despite all the changes wrought in the past two years. "It air me," he said, jocosely.

From his hollow eyes and sunken cheeks and wan smile her gaze fell upon his empty sleeve. She suddenly threw her arm across her face. "I—I—can't abide ter look at ye!" she faltered, with a gush of tears.

He stood dumfounded for a moment.

"Durn it!" he cried. "I can't abide ter look at myself!"

And with a bitter laugh he turned on his heel.

He would not be reconciled later.

The wound she had unintentionally dealt him rankled long. He said Delia Noakes was a sensible girl. Plenty of brave fellows would come home from the war, hale and hearty and with two good arms, better men in every way, in mind and body and heart and soul, for the stern experiences they were enduring so stanchly. The crop of sweethearts promised to be indeed particularly fine, and there was no use in wasting politeness on a fellow with whom she used to play before either of them could walk, but whose arm was gone now, through no glorious deed wrought for his country, for which he had intended to do all such service as a man's right arm might compass, but because he was a fool, and had made a friend of a malevolent scoundrel, who had nearly taken his life, but had only—worse luck—taken his right arm! And besides he had seen enough of the world in his wanderings to know that it behooves people to look to the future and means of support. He had learned what it was to be hungry, he had learned what it was to lack. He was no longer the brave and warlike man-at-arms, "Baby Bunting." He had no vocation, no possibility of a future of usefulness; he could not hold a gun or a plow or an ax, and Delia doubtless thought he would not be able to provide for her. And "dead shot" though he had been he could not now defend himself, he declared bitterly, much less her.

CHAPTER III

It was the last month of the year, and the month was waning. The winds had rifled the woods and the sere leaves all had fallen. Yet still a bright after-thought of the autumnal sunshine glowed along the mountain spurs, for the tardy winter loitered on the way, and the silver rime that lay on the black frost-grapes melted at a beam.

"The weather hev been powerful onseasonable an' onreasonable, ter my mind," said old Jonas Scruggs, accepting a rickety chair in his neighbor's porch. "'Tain't healthy."

"Waal, 'tain't goin' ter last," rejoined Mrs. Knox, from the doorway, where she sat with her knitting.

"'Twar jes' ter-day I seen my old gray cat run up that thar saplin' an' hang by her claws with her head down-'ards. An' I hev always knowed ez that air a sure sign of a change."

Presently she added, "The fire air treadin' snow now."

She glanced over her shoulder at the deep chimney-place, where a dull wood fire was sputtering fitfully with a sound that suggested footfalls crunching on a crust of snow.

"I dunno ez *I* need be a-hankerin' fur a change in the weather, cornsiderin' the rheumatiz in my shoulder ez I kerried around with me ez a constancy las' winter," remarked Jonas Scruggs, pre-empting a grievance in any event.

"Thar's the wild geese a-sailin' south," Hilary said, in a low, melancholy drawl, as he smoked his pipe, lounging idly on the step of the porch.

His mother laid her knitting in her lap and gazed over her spectacles into the concave vault of the sky, so vast as seen from the vantage ground of the little log cabin on the mountain's brow. Bending to the dark, wooded ranges encircling the horizon, it seemed of a crystalline transparency and of wonderful gradations of color. The broad blue stretches overhead merged into a delicate green of exquisite purity, and thence issued a suffusion of the faintest saffron in which flakes of orange burned like living fire. A jutting spur intercepted the sight of the sinking sun, and with its dazzling disk thus screened, upon the brilliant west might be descried the familiar microscopic angle speeding toward the south. A vague clamor floated downward.

"Them *fowels*, sure enough!" she said. "Sence I war a gal I hev knowed 'em by thar flyin' always in that thar peaked p'int."

"They keep thar alignment ez reg'lar," said her son suddenly, "jes' like we-uns hev ter do in the army. They hev actially got thar markers. Look at 'em dress thar ranks! An' thar's even a sergeant-major standin' out ez stiff an' percise—see him! Thar! Column forward! Guide left! March!" he cried delightedly.

"I 'lowed, Hilary, ez ye hed in an' about hed enough o' the army," said the guest, bluntly.

Hilary's face changed. But for some such reminder he sometimes forgot that missing right hand. He made no answer, his moody eyes fastened on that aërial marshaling along the vast plain of the sunset. His right arm was gone, and the stump dangled helplessly with its superfluity of brown jeans sleeve bound about it.

"Now that air a true word!" exclaimed Mrs. Knox, "only Hil'ry won't hev it so. *I* 'lows ter him ez he los' his arm through jinin' the Confed' army, an' *he* 'lows 'twar gittin' in a fight with one o' his own comrades."

Jonas Scruggs glanced keenly at her from under his bushy, grizzled eyebrows, his lips solemnly puckered, and his stubbly pointed chin resting on his knotty hands, which were clasped upon his stout stick. He had the dispassionate, pondering aspect of an umpire, which seemed to invite the cheerful submission of differences.

"Ye knows I war fur the Union, an' so war his dad," she continued. "My old man had been ailin' ennyhows, but this hyar talk o' bustin' up the Union—why, it jes' fairly harried him inter his grave. An' I 'lowed ez Hil'ry would be fur the Union, too, like everybody in the mountings ez hed good sense. But when a critter-company o' Confeds rid up the mounting one day Hil'ry he talked with some of 'em, an' he war stubborn ever after. An' so he jined the critter-company."

She fell suddenly silent, and taking up her needles knitted a row or two, her absorbed eyes, kindling with retrospection, fixed on the far horizon, for Mrs. Knox was in a position to enjoy the melancholy pleasures of a true prophet of evil, and although she had never specifically forewarned Hilary of the precise nature of the disaster that had ensued upon his enlistment, she had sought to defer and prevent it, and at last had consented only because she felt she must. She had her own secret satisfaction that the result was no worse; it lacked much of the ghastly horrors that she had foreboded—death itself, or the terrible uncertainty of hoping against hope, and fearing the uttermost dread that must needs abide with those to whom the "missing" are dear. Never now could the fact be worse, and thus she could reconcile herself, and talk of it with a certain relish of finality, as of a chapter of intense and painful interest but closed forever.

The old man nodded his head with deliberative gravity until she recommenced, when he relapsed into motionless attention.

"An' Hil'ry fought in a heap o' battles, and got shot a time or two, an' war laid up in the horspital, an' kem out cured, an' fought agin. An' one day he got inter a quar'l with one o' his bes' frien's. They war jes' funnin' afust, an' Hil'ry hit him harder'n he liked, an' he got mad, an' bein' a horseback he kicked Hil'ry. An' Hil'ry jumped on him ez suddint ez a painter, ter pull him out'n his saddle an' drub him.

Hil'ry never drawed no shootin' irons nor nuthin', an' warn't expectin' ter hurt him serious. But this hyar Jack Bixby he war full o' liquor an' fury; he started his horse a-gallopin', an' ez Hil'ry hung on ter the saddle he drawed his bowie-knife an' slashed Hil'ry's arm ez war holdin' ter him agin an' agin, till they war both soakin' in blood, an' at last Hil'ry drapped. An' the arm fevered, an' the surgeon tuk it off. An' so Hil'ry hed his discharge gin him, sence the Confeds hed no mo' use fur him. An' he walked home, two hunderd mile, he say."

During this recital the young mountaineer gave no indication of its effect upon him, and offered no word of correction to conform the details to the facts. His mother had so often told his story with the negligence of the domestic narrator, that little by little it had become thus distorted, and he knew from experience that should he interfere to alter a phase, another as far from reality would be presently substituted, for Mrs. Knox cared little how the event had been precipitated, or for aught except that his arm was gone, that he was well, and that she had him at home again, from which he should no more wander, for she had endeavored to utilize the misfortune to reinforce her authority, and illustrate her favorite dogma of the infallibility of her judgment.

Her words must have renewed bitter reminiscences, but his face was impassive, and not a muscle stirred as he silently watched the ranks of the migrating birds fade into the furthest distance.

"An' now Hil'ry thinks it air cur'ous ez I ain't sorrowin' 'bout'n his arm," she continued. "Naw, sir! I'm glad he escaped alive an' that he can't fight no mo'—not ef the war lasts twenty year, an' it 'pears like it air powerful persistin'."

It still raged, but to the denizens of this sequestered district there seemed little menace in its fury. They could hear but an occasional rumor, like the distant rumbling of thunder, and discern, as it were, a vague, transient glimmer as token of the fierce and scathing lightnings far away desolating and destroying all the world beyond these limits of peace.

Episodes of civilized warfare were little dreaded by the few inhabitants of the mountains, the old men, the women and the children, so dominated were they by the terrors of vagrant bands of stragglers and marauders, classed under the generic name of bushwhackers, repudiated by both armies, and given over to the plunder of non-combatants of both factions in this region of divided allegiance. At irregular intervals they infested this neighborhood, foraging where they listed, and housing themselves in the old hotel.

Looking across the gorge from where the three sat in the cabin porch, there was visible on the opposite heights a great white frame building, many-windowed and with wide piazzas. There were sulphur springs hard by, and before the war the place was famous as a health resort. Now it was a melancholy spectacle—silent, tenantless, vacant—infinitely lonely in the vast wilderness. Some of the doors, wrenched from their hinges, had served the raiders for fuel. The glass had been wantonly broken in many of the windows by the jocose thrusts of a saber. The grassy square within surrounded by the buildings was overgrown with weeds, and here lizards basked, and in their season wild things nested.

There was never a suggestion of the gayeties of the past—only in the deserted old ball-room when a slant of sunshine would fall athwart the dusty floor, a bluebottle might airily zigzag in the errant gleam, or when the moon was bright on the long piazzas a cobweb, woven dense, would flaunt out between the equidistant shadows of the columns like the flutter of a white dress. The place had a weird aspect, and was reputed haunted. The simple mountaineers did not venture within it, and the ghosts had it much of the time to themselves.

The obscurities of twilight were presently enfolded about it. The white walls rose, vaguely glimmering, against the pine forests in the background, and above the shadowy abysses which it overlooked.

The old man was gazing meditatively at it as he said, reprehensively,

"'Pears like ter me, Hil'ry, ez ye oughter be thankful ye warn't killed utterly—ye oughter be thankful it air no wuss."

"Hil'ry ain't thankful fur haffen o' nuthin'," Mrs. Knox interposed. "'Twar jes' las' night he looked like su'thin' in a trap. He walked the floor till nigh day—till I jes' tuk heart o' grace an' told him ez his dad hed laid them puncheons ter last, an' not to be walked on till they were wore thinner'n a clapboard in one night. An' yit he air alive an' hearty, an' I hev got my son agin. An' I sets ez much store by him with one arm ez two."

And indeed she looked cheerfully about the dusky landscape as she rose, rolling the sock on her needles and thrusting them into the ball of yarn. Old Jonas Scruggs hesitated when she told him alluringly that she had a "mighty nice ash cake kivered on the h'a'th," but he said that his daughter-in-law, Jerusha, would be expecting him, and he could in no wise bide to supper. And finally he started homeward a little wistful, but serene in the consciousness of having obeyed the behests of Jerusha, who in these hard times had grown sensitive about his habit of taking meals with his friends. "As ef," she argued, "I fed ye on half rations at home."

Hilary rose at last from the doorstep, and turning slowly to go within, his absent glance swept the night-shadowed scene. He paused suddenly, and his heart seemed beating in his throat.

A point of red light had sprung up in the vague glooms. A will-o'-the-wisp? —some wavering "ghost's candle" to light him to his grave. With his accurate knowledge of the locality he sought to place it. The distant gleam seemed to shine from a window of the old hotel, and this bespoke the arrival of rude occupants. He heard a wild halloo, a snatch of song perhaps—or was it fancy? And were the iterative echoes in the gorge the fancy of the stern old crags?

For the first time since he returned, maimed and helpless, and a non-combatant, were the lawless marauders quartered at the old hotel.

He stood for a while gazing at it with dilated eyes. Then he silently stepped within the cabin and barred the door with his uncertain and awkward left hand.

The cheerful interior of the house was all aglow. The fire had been mended, and yellow flames were undulating about the logs with many a gleaming line of grace. Blue and purple and scarlet flashes they showed in fugitive iridescence. They illumined his face, and his mother noted its pallor—the deep pallor which he had brought from the hospital.

"Ye hev got yer fancies ag'in," she cried. Then with anxious curiosity, "Whar be yer right hand now, Hil'ry?"

She alluded to that cruel hallucination of sensation in an amputated arm.

"Whar it oughter be," he groaned; "on the trigger o' my carbine."

His grief was not only that his arm was gone. It was to recognize the fact that his heart no longer beat exultantly at the mere prospect of conflict. And he was anguished with the poignant despair of a helpless man who has once been foremost in the fight.

The next day he was moody and morose, and brooded silently over the fire. The doors were closed, for winter had come at last. The hoar frost whitened the great gaunt limbs of the trees, and lay in every curled dead leaf on the ground, and followed the zig-zag lines of the fence, and embossed the fodder stack and the ash-hopper and the roofs with fantastic incongruities in silver tracery.

The sun did not shine, the clouds dropped lower and lower still, a wind sprung up, and presently the snow was flying.

The widow esteemed this as in the nature of a special providence, since the dizzying whirl of white flakes veiled the little cabin and its humble surroundings from the observation of the free-booting tenants of the old hotel across the gorge. "It air powerful selfish, I know, ter hope the bush-whackers will forage on somebody else's poultry an' sech, but somehows my own chickens seem nigher kin ter me than other folkses' be. I never see no sech ten-toed chickens ez mine nowhar.''

Reflecting further upon the peculiar merits of these chickens, ten-toed, being Dorking, reinforced by the claims of consanguinity, she presently evolved as a precautionary measure a scheme of concealing them in the "roof-room" of the cabin. And from time to time, as the silent day wore on, like the blast of a bugle the crow of a certain irrepressible young rooster demonstrated how precarious was his retirement in the loft.

"Hear the insurance o' that thar fow*ell!*" she would exclaim in exasperation. "S'pose'n the bushwhackers war hyar now, axin fur poultry, an' I war a-tellin' 'em, ez smilin' an' mealy-mouthed ez I could, that we hain't got no fow*els!* That thar reckless critter would be in the fryin'-pan 'fore night.

They'll l'arn ye ter hold yer jaw, I'll be bound!"

But the bushwhackers did not come, and the next day the veil of the falling snow still interposed, and the familiar mountains near at hand, and the long reaches of the unexplored perspective were all obscured; the drifts deepened, and the fence seemed dwarfed half covered as it was, and the boles of the trees hard by were burlier, bereft of their accustomed height. The storm ceased late one afternoon; over the white earth was a somber gray sky, but all along the horizon above the snowy summits of the western mountains a slender scarlet line betokened a fair morrow.

Hilary, in the weariness of inaction, had taken note of the weather, and with his hat drawn down over his brow he strolled out to the verge of the precipice.

THE BUSHWHACKERS

Overlooking the familiar landscape, he detected an unaccustomed smoke visible a mile or more down the narrow valley. Although but a tiny, hazy curl in the distance, it did not escape the keen eyes of the mountaineer. He could not distinguish tents against the snow, but the location suggested a camp.

The bushwhackers still lingered at the old hotel across the gorge. He could already see in the gathering dusk the firelight glancing fitfully against the window. He wondered if it were visible as far as the camp in the valley.

He stood for a long time, gazing across the snowy steeps at the desolate old building, with the heavy pine forests about it and the crags below— their dark faces seamed with white lines wherever a drift had lodged in a cleft or the interlacing tangles of icy vines might cling. In the pallid dreariness of the landscape and the gray dimness of the hovering night the lighted window blazed with the lambent splendors of some great yellow topaz. His uncontrolled fancy was trespassing upon the scene within. His heart was suddenly all a-throb with keen pain. His idle, vague imaginings of the stalwart horsemen and what they were now doing had revived within him that insatiate longing for the martial life which he had loved, that ineffable grief for the opportunity of brave deeds of value which he felt he had lost.

The drill had taught him the mastery of his muscles, but those more potent forces, his impulses, had known no discipline. A wild inconsequence now possessed him. He took no heed of reason, of prudence. He was dominated by the desire to look in upon the bushwhackers from without—they would never know—undiscovered, unimagined, like some vague and vagrant specter that might wander forlorn in the labyrinthine old house.

With an alert step he turned and strode away into the little cabin. It was very cheerful around the hearth, and the first words he heard reminded him of the season.

His younger brother, a robust lad of thirteen, was drawling reminiscences of other and happier Christmas-tides.

"Sech poppin' o' guns ez we-uns used ter hev!" said the tow-headed boy, listlessly swinging his heels against the rungs of the chair.

"The Lord knows thar's enough poppin' of guns now!" said his mother. She stooped to insert a knife under the baking hoe-cake for the purpose of turning it, which she did with a certain deft and agile flap, difficult of acquirement and impossible to the uninitiated.

"I 'members," she added, vivaciously, "we-uns used ter always hev a hollow log charged with powder an' tech it off fur the Chris'mus. It sounded like thunder—like the cannon the folks hev got nowadays."

"An' hawg-killin' times kem about the Chris'mus," said the boy, sustaining his part in the fugue.

"Folks *had* hawgs ter kill in them days," was his mother's melancholy rejoinder as she meditated on the contrast of the pinched penury of the present with the peace and plenty of the past when there was no war nor rumor of war.

"Ef ye git a hawg's bladder an' blow it up an' tie the eend right tight an' stomp on it suddint it will crack ez loud!" said the noise-loving boy. "Peas air good ter rattle in 'em, too," he added, with a wistful smile, dwelling on the clamors of his happy past.

"Waal, folks ez hed good sense seen more enjyement in eatin' spare-ribs an' souse an' sech like hawg-meat than in stomping on hawgs' bladders. I hev never favored hawg-killin' times jes' ter gin a noisy boy the means ter keep Christian folks an' church members a-jumpin' out'n thar skins with suddint skeer all the Chris'mus."

This was said with the severity of a personality, but the boy's face distended as he listened.

Suddenly his eyes brightened with excitement. "Hil'ry," he cried, joyously, "be you-uns a-goin' ter fire that thar pistol off fur the Chris'mus?"

Mrs. Knox rose from her kneeling posture on the hearth and stared blankly at Hilary.

He had come within the light of the fire. His eyes were blazing, his pale cheeks flushed, his long, lank figure was tense with energy. The weapon in his hand glittered as he held it at arm's length.

"Bein' ez it air ready loaded I reckon mebbe I ain't so awk'ard yit but I could make out ter fire it ef I war cornered," he muttered, as if to himself. "Leastwise, I'll take it along fur company."

"Air ye goin' ter fire it 'kase this be Chris'mus eve?" she asked in doubt.

He glanced absently at her and said not a word.

The next moment he had sprung out of the door and they heard his step crunching through the frozen crust of snow as he strode away.

There were rifts in the clouds and the moon looked out. The white, untrodden road lay, a glittering avenue, far along the solitudes of the dense and leafless forests. Sometimes belts of vapor shimmered before him, and as he went he saw above them the distant gables of the old hotel rising starkly against the chill sky. In view presently in the white moonlight were the long piazzas of the shattered old building, the shadows of the many tall pillars distinct upon the floor. He heard the sound of the sentry's tread, and down the vista between the columns and the shadowy colonnade he saw the soldierly figure pacing slowly to and fro.

He had not reckoned on this precaution on the part of the bushwhackers. But the rambling old building, in every nook and cranny, was familiar to him. While the sentry's back was turned, he silently crept along the piazza to an open passageway which led to the grassy square within.

The rime on the dead weeds glistened in the moonbeams; the snow lay trampled along the galleries on which opened the empty rooms; here and there, as the doors swung on their hinges, he could see through the desolate void within, the bleak landscape beyond. There were horses stabled in some of them, and in the center of the square two or three were munching their feed from the old music-stand, utilized as a manger. One of them, a handsome bay, arched his glossy neck to gaze at the intruder over the gauzy sheen of gathering vapor, his full dilated eyes with the moonlight in them. Then with a snort he went back to his corn.

Only one window was alight. There was a roaring fire within, and the ruddy glow danced on the empty walls and on the hilarious, bearded faces grouped about the hearth. The men, clad in butternut jeans, smoked their pipes as they sat on logs or lounged at length on the floor. A festive canteen was a prominent adjunct of the scene, and was often replenished from a burly keg in the corner.

As Hilary approached the window he suddenly recognized a face which he had cause to remember. He had not seen this face since Jack Bixby looked furiously down from his saddle, hacking the while with his bowie-knife at his comrade's bleeding right arm. No enemy had done this thing—Hilary's own fast friend.

He divined readily enough that after this dastardly deed Bixby had not dared to seek to rejoin Captain Bertley's squadron, and thus had found kindred spirits among this marauding band of bushwhackers. His face was not flushed with liquor now—twice the canteen passed Jack Bixby unheeded. His big black hat was thrust far back on his shock of red hair; he held his great red beard meditatively in one hand, while the other fluttered the pages of a letter. He slowly read aloud, in a droning voice, now and then, from the ill-spelled scrawl. He looked up sometimes laughing, and they all laughed in sympathy.

"'Pete Blake he axed 'bout ye, an' sent his respec's, an' Jerry Dunders says tell ye 'Howdy' fur him, though ye be fightin' on the wrong side.'"

"Jerry," he explained in a conversational tone, "he jined the Loyal Tennesseans over yander in White County."

He jerked his thumb over his shoulder westward, and one of the men said that he had known Jerry since he was "knee-high ter a duck."

In a strained, unnatural tone Jack Bixby laboriously read on.

"'Little Ben prays at night fur you. He prayed some last night out'n his own head. He said he prayed the good Lord would deliver daddy from all harm.' "

The man's eyes were glistening. He laughed hurriedly, but he coughed, too, and the comrade who knew Jerry at so minute a size seemed also acquainted with little Ben, and said a "pearter young one" had never stepped. " 'He prayed the good Lord would deliver daddy from all harm,' " Jack Bixby solemnly repeated as he folded the letter. And silence fell upon the group.

Hilary, strangely softened, was turning—he was quietly slipping away from the window when he became suddenly aware that there were other stealthy figures in the square, and he saw through the frosty panes the scared face of the sentry bursting into the doorway with a tardy alarm.

There was a rush from the square. Pistol shots rang out sharp on the chill air, and the one-armed man, conscious of his helpless plight, entrapped in the mêlée, fled as best he might through the familiar intricacies of the old hotel— up the stairs, through echoing halls and rooms, and down a long corridor, till he paused panting and breathless in the door of the old ball-room.

The rude, unplastered, whitewashed walls were illumined by the moonlight, for all down one side of the long apartment the windows overlooking the gorge were full of the white radiance, and in glittering squares it lay upon the floor.

He remembered suddenly that there was no other means of egress. To be found here was certain capture. As he turned to retrace his way he heard swift steps approaching. Guided by the sound of his flight one of the surprised party had followed him, lured by the hope of escape.

There was evidently a hot pursuit in the rear.   Now and then the long halls reverberated with pistol shots, and a bullet buried itself in the door as Jack Bixby burst into the room.   He stared aghast at his old comrade for an instant. Then as he heard the rapid footfalls, the jingle of spurs, the clamor of voices behind him, he ran to one of the windows.   He drew back dismayed by the sight of the depths of the gorge below. He was caught as in a trap.

Hilary Knox could never account for the inspiration of that moment.

At right angles with the loftier main building a one-story wing jutted out, and the space within its gable roof and above its ceiling, which was on a level with the floor of the ball-room, was separated from that apartment only by a rude screen of boards.

Hilary burst one of these rough boards loose at the lower end, and held it back with the left hand spared him.

"Jump through, Jack!" he cried out to his old enemy. "Jump through the plaster o' the ceilin' right hyar. The counter in the bar-room down thar will break yer fall."

Jack Bixby sprang through the dark aperture. There was a crash within as the plaster fell.

The next moment a bullet whizzed through Hilary's hat, and the ball-room was astir with armed men; among them Hilary recognized other mountaineers, old friends and neighbors who had joined the "Loyal Tennesseans."

"I never would hev thought ye would hev let Jack Bixby git past ye arter the way he treated ye," one of them remarked, when the search had proved futile.

"Waal," said Hilary, miserably, "I

hain't hed much grit nohows sence the surgeon took off my arm."

His interlocutor looked curiously at the hole in the young fellow's hat, pierced while he stood his ground that another man might escape. Hilary had no nice sense of discrimination. His idea of courage was the onslaught.

The others crowded about, and Hilary relished the suggestions of military comradeship that clung about them, albeit they were of the opposing faction, for they seemed so strangely cordial. Each must needs shake his hand—his awkward left hand—and he was patted on the back, and one big, bluff soul, who beamed on him with a broadly delighted smile, gave him a severe hug, such as a fatherly bear might administer.

"Hil'ry ain't got much grit, he says," one of them remarked with a guffaw. "He jes' helped another feller escape whut he hed a grudge agin, while he stood ez onconsarned ez a target, an' I shot him through the hat an' the ball ploughed up his scalp in good fashion. Glad my aim warn't a leetle mended."

Hilary's hat was gone; one of the men persisted in an exchange, and Hilary wore now a fresh new one instead of that so hastily snatched from him as a souvenir.

He thought they were all sorry for him because of the loss of his arm; yet this was strange, for many men had lost limb and life at the hands of this troop, which was of an active and bloody reputation. He could not dream they thought him a hero— these men accustomed to deeds of daring! He had no faint conception of the things they were saying of him to one another, of his gallantry and his high and noble courage in risking his life that his personal enemy might escape, when there was a chance for but one—his false friend, who had destroyed his right arm—as they mounted their horses and rode away to their camp in the valley with the prisoners they had taken.

Hilary stood listening wistfully to the jingling of their spurs and the clanking of their sabers and the regular beat of the hoofs of the galloping troop—sounds from out the familiar past, from thrilling memories, how dear!

Then as he plodded along the lonely wintry way homeward he was dismayed to reflect upon his own useless, maimed life—upon what he had suffered and what he had done.

"What ailed me ter let him off?" he exclaimed in amaze. "What ailed me ter help him git away—jes' account o' the word o' a w'uthless brat.

Fur *me* ter let *him* off when I hed my chance ter pay my grudge so slick!"

He paused on the jagged verge of a crag and looked absently over the vast dim landscape, bounded by the snowy ranges about the horizon. Here and there mists hovered above the valley, but the long slant of the moonbeams pervaded the scene and lingered upon its loneliness with luminous melancholy. The translucent amber sphere was sinking low in the vaguely violet sky, and already the dark summits of the westward pines showed a fibrous glimmer.

In the east a great star was quivering, most radiant, most pellucid. He gazed at it with sudden wistfulness. Christmas dawn was near—and this was the herald of redemption. So well it was for him that science had never invaded these skies! His simple faith beheld the Star of Bethlehem that the wise men saw when they fell down and worshiped. He broke from his moody regrets—ah, surely, of all the year this was the time when a child's prayer should meet most gracious heed in heaven, should most prevail on earth! His heart was stirred with a strange and solemn thrill, and he blessed the impulse of forgiveness for the sake of a little child.

A roseate haze had gathered about the star, deepening and glowing till the sun was in the east, and the splendid Day, charged with the sanctities of commemoration, with the fulfillment of prophecy, with the promises of all futurity, came glittering over the mountains.

But the sun was a long way off, and its brilliancy made scant impression on the intense cold. Thus it was he noticed, as he came in sight of home, that, despite the icy atmosphere, the cabin door was ajar. It moved uncertainly, yet no wind stirred.

"Thar's somebody ahint the door ez hev seen me a-comin' an' air waitin' ter ketch me 'Chris'mus Gift,'" he argued, astutely.

To forestall this he took a devious path through the brush, sprang suddenly upon the porch, thrust in his arm, and clutched the unwary party ambushed behind the door.

"Chris'mus Gift!" he shouted, as he burst into the room.

But it was Delia waiting for him, blushing and embarrassed, and seeming nearer tears than laughter. And his mother was chuckling in enjoyment of the situation.

"Now, whyn't ye let Dely ketch you-uns Chris'mus Gift like she counted on doin', stiddier ketchin' her? She hain't got nuthin' ter gin yer fur Chris'mus Gift but herself."

Hilary knew her presence here and the enterprise of "catching him Christmas Gift" was another overture at reconciliation, but when he said, "Waal, I'll thank ye kindly, Dely," she still looked at him in silence, with a timorous eye and a quivering lip.

"But, law!" exclaimed Mrs. Knox, still laughing, "I needn't set my heart on dancin' at the weddin'. Dely ain't no ways ter be trusted. She hev done like a Injun-giver afore now. Mebbe she'll take herself away from ye agin."

Delia found her voice abruptly.

"No—I won't, nuther!" she said, sturdily.

And thus it was settled.

They made what Christmas cheer they could, and he told them of a new plan as they sat together round the fire. The women humored it as a sick fancy. They never thought to see it proved.

At the school held at irregular intervals before the war he had picked up a little reading and a smattering of writing. This Christmas day he began anew. He manufactured ink of logwood that had been saved for dyeing, and the goose lent him a quill. An old blank book, thrown aside when the hotel proprietors had removed their valuables, served as paper.

As his mother had said it was not Hilary's nature to be thankful for the half of anything; he attacked the unpromising future with that undismayed ardor that had distinguished him in those cavalry charges in which he had loved to ride. With practice his left hand became deft; before the war was over he was a fair scribe, and he often pridefully remarked that he could n't be flanked on spelling. Removing to one of the valley towns, seeking a sphere of wider usefulness, his mental qualities and sterling character made themselves known and his vocation gradually became assured. He was first elected register of the county of his new home, and later clerk of the circuit court. Other preferments came to him, and the world went well with him. It became broader to his view and of more gracious aspect; his leisure permitted reading and reading fostered thought. He learned that there are more potent influences than force, and he recognized as the germ of these benignities that impulse of peace and good will which he consecrated for the sake of One who became as a Little Child.

THE PANTHER
OF
JOLTON'S RIDGE

THE PANTHER

OF

JOLTON'S RIDGE

CHAPTER I

A certain wild chasm, cut deep into the very heart of a spur of the Great Smoky Mountains, is spanned by a network, which seen from above is the heavy interlacing timbers of a railroad bridge thrown across the narrow space from one great cliff to the other, but seen from the depths of the gorge below it seems merely a fantastic gossamer web fretting the blue sky.

It often trembles with other sounds than the reverberating mountain thunder and beneath other weight than the heavy fall of the mountain rain. Trains flash across it at all hours of the night and day; in the darkness the broad glare of the head-light and the flying column of pursuing sparks have all the scenic effect of some strange uncanny meteor, with the added emphasis of a thunderous roar and a sulphurous smell; in the sunshine there skims over it at intervals a cloud of white vapor and a swift black shadow.

"Sence they hev done sot up that thar bridge I hain't seen a bar nor a deer in five mile down this hyar gorge. An' the fish don't rise nuther like they uster do. That thar racket skeers 'em."

And the young hunter, leaning upon his rifle, his hands idly clasped over its muzzle, gazed with disapproving eyes after the flying harbinger of civilization as it sped across the airy structure and plunged into the deep forest that crowned the heights.

PANTHER OF JOLTON'S RIDGE

Civilization offered no recompense to the few inhabitants of the gorge for the exodus of deer and bear and fish. It passed swiftly far above them, seeming to traverse the very sky. They had no share in the world; the freighted trains brought them nothing—not even a newspaper wafted down upon the wind; the wires flashed no word to them. The picturesque situation of the two or three little log-houses scattered at long intervals down the ravine; the crystal clear flow of a narrow, deep stream—merely a silver thread as seen from the bridge above; the grand proportions of the towering cliffs, were calculated to cultivate the grace of imagination in the brakemen, leaning from their respective platforms; to suggest a variation in the Pullman conductor's jaunty formula, "'Twould hurt our feelings pretty badly to fall over there, I fancy," and to remind the out-looking passenger of the utter loneliness of the vast wilds penetrated by the railroad. But they left no speculations behind them. The terrible sense of the inconceivable width of the world was spared the simple-minded denizens of the woods. The clanging, crashing trains came like the mountain storms, no one knew whence, and went no one knew whither. The universe lay between the rocky walls of the ravine. Even this narrow stage had its drama.

In the depths of the chasm spanned by the bridge there stood in the shadow of one of the great cliffs a forlorn little log hut, so precariously perched on the ledgy slope that it might have seemed the nest of some strange bird rather than a human habitation. The huge natural column of the crag rose sheer and straight two hundred feet above it, but the descent from the door, though sharp and steep, was along a narrow path leading in zig-zag windings amid great bowlders and knolls of scraggy earth, pushing their way out from among the stones that sought to bury them, and fragments of the cliff fallen long ago and covered with soft moss. The path appeared barely passable for man, but upon it could have been seen the imprint of a hoof, and beside the hut was a little shanty, from the rude window of which protruded a horse's head, with so interested an expression of countenance that he looked as if he were assisting at the conversation going on out-of-doors this mild March afternoon.

"Ye could find deer, an' bar, an' sech, easy enough ef ye would go arter 'em," replied the young hunter's mother, as she sat in the doorway knitting a yarn sock. "That thar still-house up yander ter the Ridge hev skeered off the deer an' bar fur ye worse'n the railroad hev. Ye kin git that fur an' no furder. Ye hev done got triflin' an' no 'count, an' nuthin' else in this worl' ails ye,—nur the deer an' bar, nuther," she concluded, with true maternal candor.

"It war tole ter me," said an elderly man, who was seated in a rush-bottomed chair outside the door, and who, although a visitor, bore a lance in this domestic controversy with much freedom and spirit, "ez how ye hed done got religion up hyar ter the Baptis' meetin'-house the last revival ez we hed. An' I s'posed it war the truth."

"I war convicted," replied the young fellow, ambiguously, still leaning lazily on his rifle. He was a striking figure, remarkable for a massive proportion and muscular development, and yet not lacking the lithe, elastic curves characteristic of first youth. A dilapidated old hat crowned a shock of yellow hair, a sunburned face, far-seeing gray eyes, and an expression of impenetrable calm. His butternut suit was in consonance with the prominent ribs of his horse, the poverty-stricken aspect of the place, and the sterile soil of a forlorn turnip patch which embellished the slope to the water's edge.

"Convicted!" exclaimed his mother, scornfully. "An' sech goin's-on sence! Mark never *hed* no religion to start with."

"What did ye see when ye war convicted?" demanded the inquisitive guest, who spoke upon the subject of religion with the authority and asperity of an expert.

"I never seen nuthin' much." Mark Yates admitted the fact reluctantly.

"Then ye never *hed* no religion,"

retorted Joel Ruggles. "I *knows*, 'kase I hev hed a power o' visions. I hev viewed heaven an' hung over hell." He solemnly paused to accent the effect of this stupendous revelation.

There had lately come a new element into the simple life of the gorge, —a force infinitely more subtle than that potency of steam which was wont to flash across the railroad bridge; of further reaching influences than the wide divergences of the civilization it spread in its swift flight. Naught could resist this force of practical religion applied to the workings of daily life. The new preacher that at infrequent intervals visited this retired nook had wrought changes in the methods of the former incumbent, who had long ago fallen into the listless apathy of old age, and now was dead. His successor came like a whirlwind, sweeping the chaff before him — a humble man, ignorant, poor in this world's goods, and of meager physical strength. It was in vain that the irreverent sought to bring ridicule upon him, that he was called a "skimpy saint" in reference to his low stature, "the widow's mite," a sly jest at the hero-worship of certain elderly relicts in his congregation, a "two-by-four text" to illustrate his slim proportions. He was armed with the strength of righteousness, and it sufficed.

It was much resented at first that he carried his spiritual supervision into the personal affairs of those of his charge, and required that they should make these conform to their outward profession. And thus old feuds must needs be patched up, old enemies forgiven, restitution made, and the kingdom set in order as behooves the domain of a Prince of Peace. The young people especially were greatly stirred, and Mark Yates, who had never hitherto thought much of such subjects, had experienced an awakening of moral resolve, and had even appeared one day at the mourners' bench.

Thus he had once gone up to be prayed for, "convicted of sin," as the phrase goes in those secluded regions. But the sermons were few, for the intervals were long between the visitations of the little preacher, and Mark's conscience had not learned the art of holding forth with persistence and pertinence, which spiritual eloquence (not always welcome) is soon acquired by a receptive, sensitive temperament. Mark was cheerful, light-hearted, imaginative, adaptable. The traits of the wilder, ruder element of the district, the hardy courage, the physical prowess, the adventurous escapades appealed to his sense of the picturesque as no merit of the dull domestic boor, content with the meager agricultural routine, tamed by the endless struggle with work and unalterable poverty, could stir him. He had no interest in defying the law and shared none of the profits, but the hair-breadth escapes of certain illicit distillers hard by, their perpetual jeopardy, the ingenuity of their wily devices to evade discovery by the revenue officers and yet supply all the contiguous region, the cogency of their arguments as to the injustice of the taxation that bore so heavily upon the small manufacturer, their moral posture of resisting and outwitting oppression—all furnished abundant interest to a mind alert, capable, and otherwise unoccupied.

Not so blunt were his moral perceptions, however, that he did not secretly wince when old Joel Ruggles, after meditating silently, chewing his quid of tobacco, reverted from the detail of the supposed spiritual wonders, which in his ignorance he fancied he had seen, to the matter in hand:

"Hain't you-uns hearn 'bout the sermon ez the preacher hev done preached agin that thar still?—*he* called it a den o' 'niquity."

"I hearn tell 'bout'n it yander ter the still," replied Mark, calmly. "They 'lowed thar ez they hed a mind ter pull him down out'n the pulpit fur his outdaciousness, 'kase they war all thar ter the meetin'-house, an' *he* seen 'em, an' said what he said fur them ter hear." He paused, a trifle uncomfortable at the suggestion of violence. Then reassuring himself by a moment's reflection, he went on in an offhand way, "I reckon they ain't a-goin' ter do nuthin' agin *him*, but he hed better take keer how he jows at them still folks. They air a hard-mouthed generation, like the Bible says, an' they hev laid off ter stop that thar talk o' his'n.''

"Did ye hear 'em sayin' what they war a-aimin' ter do?'' asked Ruggles, keenly inquisitive.

"'Tain't fer me ter tell what I hearn whilst visitin' in other folkses' houses,'' responded the young fellow, tartly. "But I never hearn 'em say nuthin' 'ceptin' they war a-goin' ter try ter stop his talk,'' he added. "I tells ye that much 'kase ye'll be a-thinkin' I hearn worse ef I don't. That air all I hearn 'em say 'bout'n it. An' I reckon they don't mean nuthin', but air talkin' big whilst mad 'bout'n it. They air 'bleeged ter know thar goin's-on ain't fitten fur church members.''

"An' ye a-jowin' 'bout'n a hard-mouthed generation,'' interposed his mother, indignantly. "Ye're one of 'em yerself. Thar hain't been a bite of wild meat in this hyar house fur a month an' better. Mark hev' mighty nigh tucken ter live at the still; an' when he kin git hisself up to the p'int o' goin' a-huntin', 'pears like he can't find nuthin' ter shoot. I hev hearn a sayin' ez thar is a use fur every livin' thing, an' it 'pears ter me ez Mark's use air mos'ly ter waste powder an' lead.''

Mark received these sarcasms with an imperturbability which might in some degree account for their virulence and, indeed, Mrs. Yates often averred that, say what she might, she could not ''move that thar boy no more'n the mounting.''

He shifted his position a trifle, still leaning, however, upon the rifle, with his clasped hands over the muzzle and his chin resting on his hands. The quiet radiance of a smile was beginning to dawn in his clear eyes as he looked at his interlocutors, and he spoke with a confidential intonation:

"The las' meetin' but two ez they hev hed up yander ter the church they summonsed them thar Brices ter 'count fur runnin' of a still, an' a-gittin' drunk, an' sech, an' the Brices never come, nor tuk no notice nor nuthin'. An' then the nex' meetin' they tuk an' turned 'em out'n the church. An' when they hearn 'bout that at the still, them Brices—the whole lay-out—war pipin' hot 'bout'n it. Thar warn't nare member what voted fur a-keepin' of 'em in; an' that stuck in 'em, too— all thar old frien's a-goin' agin 'em! I s'pose 'twar right ter turn 'em out," he added, after a reflective pause, "though thar is them ez war a-votin' agin them Brices ez hev drunk a powerful lot o' whisky an' sech in thar lifetime."

"Thar will be a sight less whisky drunk about hyar ef that small-sized preacher-man kin keep up the holt he hev tuk on temperance sermons,'' said Mrs. Yates a trifle triumphantly. Then with a clouding brow: ''I could wish he war bigger. I ain't faultin' the ways o' Providence in nowise, but it do 'pear ter me ez one David and G'liath war enough fur the tales o' religion 'thout hevin' our own skimpy leetle shepherd and the big Philistines of the distillers at loggerheads—whenst flat peebles from the brook would be a mighty pore dependence agin a breech-loading rifle. G'liath's gun war more'n apt ter hev been jes' a old muzzle-loader, fur them war the times afore the war fur the Union; but these hyar moonshiners always hev the best an' newest shootin'-irons that Satan kin devise—not knowin' when some o' the raiders o' the revenue force will kem down on 'em—an' that makes a man keen ter be among the accepted few in the new quirks o' firearms. A mighty small man the preacher-man 'pears ter be! If it war the will o' Providence I could wish fur a few more pounds o' Christian pastor, considering the size an' weight ez hev been lavished on them distillers."

"It air scandalous fur a church member ter be a gittin' drunk an' foolin' round the still-house an' sech," said Joel Ruggles, "an' ef ye hed ever hed any religion, Mark, ye'd hev knowed that 'thout hevin' ter be told."

"An' it's scandalous fur a church member to drink whisky at all," said Mrs. Yates, sharply, knitting off her needle, and beginning another round. A woman's ideas of reform are always radical.

Joel Ruggles did not eagerly concur in this view of the abstinence question; he said nothing in reply.

"Thar hain't sech a mighty call ter

drink whisky yander ter the still,"
remarked young Yates, irrelevantly,
feeling perhaps the need of a plea of
defense. "It ain't the whisky ez
draws me thar. The gang air a-hangin' round an' a-talkin' an' a-laughin'
an' a-tellin' tales 'bout bar-huntin' an'
sech. An' thar's the grist mill a haffen
mile an' better through the woods."

"Thar's bad company at the still,
an' it's a wild beast ez hev got a fang
ez bites sharp an' deep, an' some day
ye'll feel it, ez sure ez ye're a born
sinner," said Mrs. Yates, looking up
solemnly at him over her spectacles.
"I never see no sense in men a-drinkin' of whisky," she continued, after a
pause, during which she counted her
stitches. "The wild critters in the
woods hev got more reason than ter
eat an' drink what'll pizen 'em—but,
law! it always did 'pear to me ez they
war ahead in some ways of the men,

what kin talk an' hev got the hope of salvation.''

This thrust was neither parried nor returned. Joel Ruggles, discreetly silent, gazed with a preoccupied air at the swift stream flowing far below, beginning to darken with the overhanging shadows of the western crags. And Mark still leaned his chin meditatively on his hands, and his hands on the muzzle of his rifle, in an attitude so careless that an unaccustomed observer might have been afraid of seeing the piece discharged and the picturesque head blown to atoms.

Through the futility of much remonstrance his mother had lost her patience—no great loss, it might seem, for in her mildest days she had never been meek. Poverty and age, and in addition her anxiety concerning a son now grown to manhood, good and kind in disposition, but whose very amiability rendered him so lax in his judgment of the faults of others as to slacken the tension of his judgment of his own faults, and whose stancher characteristics were manifested only in an adamantine obstinacy to her persuasion—all were ill-calculated to improve her temper and render her optimistic, and she had had no training in the wider ways of life to cultivate tact and knowledge of character and methods of influencing it. Doubtless the "skimpy saint" in the enlightenment of his vocation would have approached the subject of these remonstrances in a far different spirit, for Mark was plastic to good suggestions, easily swayed, and had no real harm in him. He understood, too, the merit and grace of consistency, of being all of a piece with his true identity, with his real character, with the sterling values he most appreciated. But the quality that rendered him so susceptible to good influences—his adaptability—exposed him equally to adverse temptation. He had spoken truly when he had said that it was only the interest of the talk of the moonshiners and their friends—stories of hunting fierce animals in the mountain fastnesses, details of bloody feuds between neighboring families fought out through many years with varying vicissitudes, and old-time traditions of the vanished Indian, once the master of all the forests and rocks and rivers of these ancient wilds— and not the drinking of whisky, that allured him; far less the painful and often disgusting exhibitions of drunkenness he occasionally witnessed at the still, in which those sufficiently sober found· a source of stupid mirth. Afterward it seemed to him strange to reflect on his course. True he had had but a scanty experience of life and the world, and the parson's reading from the Holy Scriptures was his only acquaintance with what might be termed literature or learning in any form. But arguing merely from what he knew he risked much. From the pages of the Bible he had learned what the leprosy was, and what, he asked himself in later years, would he have thought of the mental balance of a man who frequented the society of a leper for the sake of transitory entertainment or mirth to be derived from his talk? In the choice stories of "bar" and "Injuns," innocent in themselves, he must needs risk the moral contagion of this leprosy of the soul.

Nevertheless he was intent now on escaping from his mother and Joel Ruggles, since it was growing late and he knew the cronies would soon be gathered around the big copper at the still-house, and he welcomed the diversion of a change of the subject. It had fallen upon the weather—the most propitious times of plowing and planting; an earnest confirmation of the popular theory that to bring a crop potatoes and other tubers must be planted in the dark of the moon, and leguminous vegetables, peas, beans, etc., in the light of the moon. Warned by the lengthening shadows, Joel Ruggles broke from the pacific discussion of these agricultural themes, rose slowly from his chair, went within to light his pipe at the fire, and with this companion wended his way down the precipitous slope, then along the rocky banks of the stream to his own little home, half a mile or so up its rushing current.

As he went he heard Mark's clear

voice lifted in song further down the stream. He had hardly noted when the young fellow had withdrawn from the conversation. It was a mounted shadow that he saw far away among the leafy shadows of the oaks and the approaching dusk. Mark had slipped off and saddled his half-broken horse, Cockleburr, and was doubtless on his way to his boon companions at the distillery.

The old man stood still, leaning on his stick, as he silently listened to the song, the sound carrying far on the placid medium of the water and in the stillness of the evening.

"O, call the dogs—Yo he!—Yo ho!
    Boone and Ranger, Wolf an' Beau,
    Little Bob-tail an' Big Dew-claw,
    Old Bloody-Mouth an' Hanging Jaw.
    Ye hear the hawns?—Yo he!—Yo ho!
    They all are blowin', so far they go,
    With might an' main, for the trail is fresh,
    A big bear's track in the aidge o' the bresh!"

"Yo he! yo ho!" said the river

faintly. "Yo he! yo ho!" said the rocks more faintly; and fainter still from the vague darkness came an echo so slight that it seemed as near akin to silence as to sound, barely impinging upon the air. "Yo he! yo ho!" it murmured.

But old Joel Ruggles, standing and listening, silently shook his head and said nothing.

"Yo he! yo ho!" sung Mark, further away, and the echoes of his boyish voice still rang vibrant and clear.

Then there was no sound but the stir of the river and the clang of the iron-shod hoofs of Cockleburr, striking the stones in the rocky bridle-path. The flint gave out a flash of light, the yellow spark glimmering for an instant, visible in the purple dusk with a transitory flicker like a firefly.

And old Joel Ruggles once more shook his head.

CHAPTER II

Far away in a dim recess of the deep woods, on the summit of the ridge, amidst crags and chasms and almost inaccessible steeps, the shadows had gathered about a dismal little log hut of one room—like all the other dismal little hovels of the mountain, save that in front of the door the grass was worn away from a wide space by the frequent tread of many feet; a preternaturally large wood-pile was visible under a frail shelter in the rear of the house; from the chimney a dense smoke rose in a heavy column; and the winds that rushed past it carried on their breath an alcoholic aroma. But for these points of dissimilarity and its peculiarly secluded situation,

PANTHER OF JOLTON'S RIDGE

Mark Yates, dismounting from his restive steed, might have been entering his mother's dwelling. The opening door shed no glare of firelight out into the deepening gloom of the dusk. It was very warm within, however—almost too warm for comfort; but the shutters of the glassless window were tightly barred, and the usual chinks of log-house architecture were effectually closed with clay. The darkness of the room was accented rather than dispelled by a flickering tallow dip stuck in an empty bottle in default of a candlestick, and there was an all-pervading and potent odor of spirits. The salient feature of the scene was a stone furnace, from the closed door of which there flashed now and then a slender thread of brilliant light. A great copper still rose from it, and a protruding spiral tube gracefully meandered away in the darkness through the cool waters of the refrigerator to the receiver of its precious condensed vapors.

There were four jeans-clad mountaineers seated in the gloomy twilight of this apartment; and the stories of "bar-huntin' an' sech" must have been very jewels of discourse to prove so alluring, as they could certainly derive no brilliancy from their unique but somber setting.

"Hy're, Mark! Come in, come in," was the hospitable insistence which greeted young Yates.

"Hev a cheer," said Aaron Brice, the eldest of the party, bringing out from the darkness a chair and placing it in the feeble twinkle of the tallow dip.

"Take a drink, Mark," said another of the men, producing a broken-nosed pitcher of ardent liquor. But notwithstanding this effusive hospitality, which was very usual at the still-house, Mark

PANTHER OF JOLTON'S RIDGE

Yates had an uncomfortable impression that he had interrupted an important conference, and that his visit was badly timed. The conversation that ensued was labored, and hosts and guest were a trifle ill at ease. Frequent pauses occurred, broken only by the sound of the furnace fire, the boiling and bubbling within the still, the gurgle of the water through its trough, that led it down from a spring on the hill behind the house to the refrigerator, the constant dripping of the "doublings" from the worm into the keg below. Now and then one of the brothers hummed a catch which ran thus:—

> "O, Eve, she gathered the pippins,
> Adam did the pomace make;
> When the brandy told upon 'em,
> They accused the leetle snake!"

Another thoughtfully snuffed the tallow dip, which for a few moments burned with a brighter, more cheerful light, then fell into a tearful despondency and bade fair to weep itself away.

Outside the little house the black night had fallen, and the wind was raging among the trees. All the stars seemed in motion, flying to board a fleet of flaky white clouds that were crossing the sky under full sail. The moon, a spherical shadow with a crescent of burnished silver, was speeding toward the west; not a gleam fell from its disk upon the swaying, leafless trees—it seemed only to make palpable the impenetrable gloom that immersed the earth. The air had grown keen and cold, and it rushed in at the door as it was opened with a wintry blast. A man entered, with the slow, lounging motion peculiar to the mountaineers, bearing in his hand a jug of jovial aspect. The four Brices looked up from under their heavy brows with sharp scrutiny to discern among the deep shadows cast by the tallow dip who the newcomer might be. Their eyes returned to gaze with an affected preoccupation upon the still, and in this significant hush the ignored visitor stood surprised and abashed on the threshold. The cold inrushing mountain wind, streaming like a jet of seawater through the open door, was rapidly lowering the temperature of the room. This contemptuous silence was too fraught with discomfort to be maintained.

"Ef ye air a-comin' in," said Aaron Brice, ungraciously, "come along in. An' ef ye air a-goin' out go 'long. Anyway, jes' ez ye choose, ef ye'll shet that thar door, ez I don't see ez ye hev any call ter hold open."

Thus adjured the intruder closed the door, placed the jug on the floor, and looked about with an embarrassed hesitation of manner. The flare from the furnace, which Aaron Brice had opened to pile in fresh wood, illumined the newcomer's face and long, loose-jointed figure and showed the semi-circle of mountaineers seated in their rush-bottomed chairs about the still. None of them spoke. Never before since the still-house was built had a visitor stood upon the puncheon floor that one of the hospitable Brices did not scuttle for a chair, that the dip was not eagerly snuffed in the vain hope of irradiating the guest, that the genial though mutilated pitcher filled with whisky was not ungrudgingly presented. No chair was offered now, and the broken-nosed pitcher with its ardent contents was motionless on the head of a barrel. It was a strange change, and as the broad red glare fell on their stolid faces and blankly inexpressive attitudes the guest looked from one to the other with an increasing surprise and a rising dismay. The light was full for a moment upon Mark Yates's shock of yellow hair, gray eyes, and muscular, well-knit figure, as he, too, sat mute among his hosts. He was not to be mistaken, and once seen was not easily forgotten. The next instant the furnace door clashed, and the room fell back into its habitual gloom. One might note only the gurgle of the spring water—telling of the wonders of the rock-barricaded earth below and the reflected glories of the sky above—only the hilarious song of the still, the continuous trickle from the worm, the all-pervading spirituous odors, and the shadowy outlines of the massive figures of the mountaineers.

The Brices evidently could not be relied upon to break the awkward silence. The newcomer, mustering heart of grace, took up his testimony in a languid nasal drawl, trying to speak and to appear as if he had noticed nothing remarkable in his reception.

"I hev come, Aaron," he said, "ter git another two gallons o' that thar whisky ez I hed from you-uns, an' I hev brung the balance of the money I owed ye on that, an' enough ter pay for the jugful, too. Hyar is a haffen dollar fur the old score, an'—"

"That thar eends it," said Aaron, pocketing the tendered fifty cents. "We air even, an' ye'll git no more whisky from hyar, Mose Carter."

"Wha—what did ye say, Aaron? I hain't got the rights 'zactly o' what ye said." And Carter peered in great amaze through the gloom at his host, who was carefully filling a pipe. As Aaron stooped to get a coal from the furnace one of the others spoke.

"He said ez ye'll git no more whisky from hyar. An' it air a true word."

The flare from the furnace again momentarily illumined the room, and as the door clashed it again fell back into the uncertain shadow.

"That is what I tole ye," said Aaron, reseating himself and puffing his pipe into a strong glow, "an' ef ye hain't a-onderstandin' of it yit I'll say it agin—ye an' the rest of yer tribe will git no more liquor from hyar."

"An' what's the reason I hain't a-goin' ter get no more liquor from hyar?" demanded Moses Carter in virtuous indignation. "Hain't I been ez good pay ez any man down this hyar gorge an' the whole mounting atop o' that? Look-a hyar, Aaron Brice, ye ain't a-goin' ter try ter purtend ez I don't pay fur the liquor ez I gits hyar—an' you-uns an' me done been a-tradin' tergither peaceable-like fur nigh on ter ten solid year."

"An' then ye squar' round an' gits

me an' my brothers a-turned out'n the church fur runnin' of a still whar ye gits yer whisky from. Good pay or bad pay, it's all the same ter me."

"I never gin my vote fur a-turnin' of ye out 'kase of ye a-runnin' of a still." Moses Carter trembled in his eager anxiety to discriminate the grounds upon which he had cast his ballot. "It war fur a-gittin' drunk an' a-stayin' drunk, ez ye mos'ly air a-doin— an' ye will 'low yerself, Aaron, ez that thar air a true word. I don't see no harm in a-runnin' of a still an' a-drinkin' some, but not ter hurt. It air this hyar gittin' drunk constant ez riles me."

"Mose Carter," said the youngest of the Brice brothers, striking suddenly into the conversation, "ye air a liar, an' ye knows it!" He was a wiry, active man of twenty-five years; he spoke in an authoritative high key, and his voice seemed to split the air like a knife. His mind was as wiry as his body, and it was generally understood on Jolton's Ridge that he was the power behind the throne of which Aaron, the eldest, wielded the unmeaning scepter; he, however, remained decorously in the background, for among the humble mountaineers the lordly rights of primogeniture are held in rigorous veneration, and it would have ill-beseemed a younger scion of the house to openly take precedence of the elder. His Christian name was John, but it had been forgotten or disregarded by all but his brothers in the title conferred upon him by his comrades of the mountain wilds. Panther Brice—or "Painter," for thus the animal is called in the vernacular of the region—was known to run the still, to shape the policy of the family, to be a self-constituted treasurer and disburser of the common fund, to own the very souls of his unresisting elder brothers. He had elected, however, in the interests of decorum, that these circumstances should be sedulously ignored. Aaron invariably appeared as spokesman, and the mountaineers at large all fell under the influence of a dominant mind and acquiesced in the solemn sham. The Panther seldom took part even in casual discussions of any vexed question, reserving his opinions to dictate as laws to his brothers in private; and a sensation stirred the coterie when his voice, that had a knack of finding and thrilling every sensitive nerve in his hearer's body, jarred the air.

"I hev seen ye, Mose Carter," he continued, "in this hyar very still-house ez drunk ez a fraish biled owl. Ye hev laid on this hyar floor too drunk ter move hand or foot all night an' haffen the nex' day at one spree. I hev seen ye', an' so hev plenty o' other folks. An' ef ye comes hyar a-jowin' so sanctified 'bout'n folks a-gittin' drunk, I'll turn ye out'n this hyar still-house fur tellin' of lies."

He paused as abruptly as he had spoken; but before Moses Carter could collect his slow faculties he had resumed. "It 'pears powerful comical ter me ter hear this hyar Baptis' church a-settin' of itself up so stiff fur temp'rance, 'kase thar air an old sayin'— an' I b'lieves it—ez the Presbyterians holler—'What is ter be will be!—even ef it won't be!' an' the Methodies holler, 'Fire! fire! fire! Brimstun' an' blue blazes!'—but the Bapties holler, 'Water! water! water! with a *leetle* drap o' whisky in it!' But ye an' yer church 'll be dry enough arter this; thar'll be less liquor drunk 'mongst ye'n ever hev been afore, 'kase ye air all too cussed stingy ter pay five cents extry a quart like ye'll hev ter do at Joe Gilligan's store down yander ter the Settlemint. Fur nare one o' them sanctified church brethren'll git another drap o' liquor hyar, whar it hev always been so powerful cheap an' handy."

"The dryer ez ye kin make the church the better ye'll please the pa'son. He lays off a reg'lar temperance drought fur them ez kin foller arter his words. I be a-tryin' ter mend my ways," Moses Carter droned with a long, sanctimonious face, "but—" he hesitated, "the sperit is willin', but the flesh is weak—the flesh is weak!"

"I'll be bound no sperits air weak ez ye hev ennything ter do with, leastwise swaller," said the Panther, with a quick snap.

"He is hyar in the mounting ternight, the pa'son," resumed Mose Carter, with that effort, always ill-starred, to affect to perceive naught amiss when a friend is sullenly belligerent; he preserved the indifferent tone of one retailing casual gossip. "The pa'son hev laid off ter spen' the better part o' the night in prayer and wrestlin' speritchully in the church-house agin his sermon ter-morrer, it bein' the blessed Sabbath. He 'lowed he would be more sole and alone thar than at old man Allen's house, whar he be puttin' up fur the night, 'kase at old man Allen's they hev seben granchil'ren an' only one room, barrin' the roof-room. Thar be a heap o' onregenerate human natur' in them seben Allen gran'chil'ren. Thar ain't no use I reckon in tryin' ter awake old man Allen ter a sense of sin an' the awful oncertainty of life by talkin' ter *him* o' the silence an' solitude o' the grave! Kee, kee!" he laughed. But he laughed alone.

"*Wrestlin'!*" The pa'son a-wrestlin'! I could throw him over my head! It's well fur him his wrestlin's air only in prayer!" exclaimed Painter, with scorn. "The still will holp on the cause o' temp'rance more'n that thar little long-tongued preacher an' all his sermons. Raisin' the tar'ff on the drink will stop it. Ye're all so dad-burned stingy."

"Jes' ez ye choose," said Moses Carter, taking up his empty jug. "'Tain't nuthin' s'prisin' ter me ter hear ye a-growlin' an' a-goin' this hyar way, Painter—ye always war more like a wild beast nor a man, anyhow. But it do 'stonish me some ez Aaron an' the t'other boys air a-goin' ter let ye cut 'em out'n a-sellin' of liquor ter the whole kentry mighty nigh, 'kase the brethren don't want a sodden drunkard, like ye air, in the church a-communin' with the saints."

PANTHER OF JOLTON'S RIDGE

"Ye needn't sorrow fur Aaron," said Panther Brice, with a sneer that showed his teeth much as a snarl might have done, "nor fur the t'other boys nuther. We kin sell all the whisky ez we kin make ter Joe Gilligan, an' the folks yander ter—ter—no matter whar—" he broke off with a sudden look of caution as if he had caught himself in an imminent disclosure. "We kin sell it 'thout losin' nare cent, fur we hev always axed the same price by the gallon ez by the bar'l. So Aaron ain't a needin' of yer sorrow."

"Ye air the spitefullest little painter ez ever seen this hyar worl'," exclaimed Moses Carter, exasperated by the symmetry of his enemy's financial scheme. "Waal—waal, prayer may bring ye light. Prayer is a powerful tool. The pa'son b'lieves in its power. He is right now up yander in the church-house, fur I seen the light, an' I hearn his voice lifted in prayer ez I kem by.''

The four brothers glanced at one another with hot, wild eyes. They had reason to suspect that they were themselves the subject of the parson's supplications, and they resented this as a liberty. They had prized their standing in the church not because they were religious, in the proper sense of the word, but from a realization of its social value. In these primitive regions the sustaining of a reputation for special piety is a sort of social distinction and a guarantee of a certain position. The moonshiners neither knew nor cared what true religion might be. To obey its precepts or to inconvenience themselves with its restraints, was alike far from their intention. They had received with boundless amazement the first intimation that the personal and practical religion which the "skimpy saint" had brought into the gorge might consistently interfere with the liquor trade, the illicit distilling of whisky, and the unlimited imbibing thereof by themselves and the sottish company that frequented the still-house. They had laughed at his temperance sermons and ridiculing his warnings had treated the whole onslaught as a trifle, a matter of polemical theory, in the nature of things transitory, and had expected it to wear out as similar spasms of righteousness often do—more's the pity! Then they would settle down to continue to furnish spirituous comfort to the congregation, while the "skimpy saint" ministered to their spiritual needs. The warlike little parson, however, had steadily advanced his parallels, and from time to time had driven the distillers from one subterfuge to another, till at last, although they were well off in this world's goods —rich men, according to the appraisement of the gorge—they were literally turned out of the church, and had become a public example, and they felt that they had experienced the most unexpected and disastrous catastrophe possible in nature.

They were stunned that so small a man had done this thing, a man, so poor, so weak, so dependent for his bread, his position, his every worldly need, on the favor of the influential members of his scattered congregations. It had placed them in their true position before their compeers. It had reduced their bluster and boastfulness. It had made them seem very small to themselves, and still smaller, they feared, in the estimation of others.

Moses Carter — himself no shining light, indeed a very feebly glimmering luminary in the congregation—looked from one to the other of their aghast indignant faces with a ready relish of the situation, and said, with a grin:

"I reckon, Painter, ef the truth war plain, ye'd ruther hev all the gorge ter know ez the pa'son war a-spreadin' the fac's about this hyar still afore a United States marshal than afore the throne o' grace, like he be a-doin' of right now."

The Panther rose with a quick, lithe motion, stretched out his hand to the head of a barrel near by, and the thread of light from the closed furnace door showed the glitter of steel. He came forward a few steps, walking with a certain sinewy grace and brandishing a heavy knife, his furious eyes gleaming with a strange green brilliance, all the more distinct in the half-darkened room. Then he paused, as with a new thought. "I won't tech ye now," he said, with a snarl, "but arter a while I'll jes' make ye 'low ez that thar church o' yourn air safer with me in it nor it air with me out'n it. An' then we'll count it even.'' He ceased speaking suddenly; cooler now, and with an expression of vexation upon his sharp features—perhaps he repented his hasty threat and his self-betrayal. After a moment he went on, but with less virulence of manner than before. ''Ye kin take that thar empty jug o' yourn an' kerry it away empty. An' ye kin take yer great hulking stack o' bones along with it, an' thank yer stars ez none of 'em air bruken. Ye air the fust man ever turned empty out'n this hyar still-house, an' I pray God ez ye may be the las', 'kase I don't want no sech wuthless cattle a-hangin' round hyar.''

''I ain't a-quarrelin' with hevin' ter go,'' retorted Carter, with asperity. ''I never sot much store by comin' hyar nohow, 'ceptin' Aaron an' me, we war toler'ble frien'ly fur a good many year. This hyar still-house always reminded me sorter o' hell, anyhow—whar the worm dieth not an' the fire is not quenched."

With this Parthian dart he left the room, closing the door after him, and presently the dull thud of his horse's hoofs was borne to the ears of the party within, again seated in a semicircle about the furnace.

CHAPTER III

After a few moments of vexed cogitation Aaron broke the silence, keeping, however, a politic curb on his speech. "'Pears ter me, John, ez how mebbe 'twould hev done better ef ye hedn't said that thar ez ye spoke 'bout'n the church-house."

"Hold yer jaw!" returned the Panther, fiercely. "Who larned ye ter jedge o' my words? An' it don't make no differ nohow. I done tole him nuthin' 'bout'n the church-house ez the whole Ridge won't say arterward, any way ez ye kin fix it."

If Mark Yates had found himself suddenly in close proximity to a real panther he could hardly have felt more uncomfortable than these half-covert suggestions rendered him. He shrank from dwelling upon what they seemed to portend, and he was anxious to hear no more. The recollection of sundry maternal warnings concerning the evils, moral and temporal, incident upon keeping bad company, came on him with a crushing weight, and transformed the aspect of the fascinating still-house into a close resemblance to another locality of worm and fire, to which the baffled Carter had referred. He was desirous of going, but feared that so early a departure just at this critical juncture might be interpreted by his entertainers as a sign of distrust and a disposition to stand aloof when they were deserted by their other friends. And yet he knew, as well as if they had told him, that his arrival had interrupted some important discussion of the plot they were laying, and they only waited his exit to renew their debate.

While these antagonistic emotions swayed him, he sat with the others in meditative silence, gazing blankly at the pleasing rotundity of the dense shadow which he knew was the "copper," and listening to the frantic dance and roistering melody of its bubbling, boiling, surging contents, to the monotonous trickling of the liquor falling from the worm, to the gentle cooing of the rill of clear spring water. The idea of pleasure suggested by the very sight of the place had given way as more serious thoughts and fears crowded in, and his boyish liking for these men who possessed that deadly fascination for youth and inexperience,—the reputation of being wild,—was fast changing to aversion. He still entertained a strong sympathy for those fierce qualities which gave so vivid an interest to the stirring accounts of struggles with wolves and wild cats, bears and panthers, and to the histories of bitter feuds between human enemies, in the bloody sequel of which, however, the brutality of the deed often vied with its prowess; but this fashion of squaring off, metaphorically speaking, at the preacher, and the strange insinuations of sacrilegious injury to the church— the beloved church, so hardly won from the wilderness, representing the rich gifts of the very poor, their time, their labor, their love, their prayers—this struck every chord of conservatism in his nature.

There had never before been a church building in this vicinity; "summer preachin' " under the forest oaks had sufficed, with sometimes at long intervals a funeral sermon at the house of a neighbor. But in response to that strenuous cry, "Be up aud doing," and in acquiescence with the sharp admonition that religion does not consist in singing sleepy hymns in a comfortable chimney-corner, the whole countryside had roused itself to the privilege of the work nearest its hand. Practical Christianity first developed at the saw-mill. The great logs, seasoned lumber from the forest, were offered as a sacrifice to the glory of God, and as the word went around, Mark Yates, always alert, was among the first of the groups that came and stood and watched the gleaming steel striking into the fine white fibers of the wood — the beginnings of the "church-house"—while the dark, clear water reflected the great beams and roof of the mill, and the sibilant whizzing of the simple machinery seemed, with the knowledge of the consecrated nature of its work, an harmonious undertone to the hymning of the pines, and the gladsome rushing of the winds, and the subdued ecstasies of all the lapsing currents of the stream.

Mark had looked on drearily. His spirit, awakened by the clarion call of duty, fretted and revolted at the restraints of his lack of means. He could do naught. It was the privilege of others to prepare the lumber. It seemed that even inanimate nature had its share in building the church—the earth in its rich nurture that had given strength to the great trees; the seasons that had filled the veins of each with the rich wine of the sap, the bourgeoning impulse of its leafage and the ripeness of its fine fruitions; the rainfall and sunshine that had fed and fostered and cherished it—only he had naught to give but the idle gaze of wistful eyes.

The miller, a taciturn man, was

very well aware that he had sawed the lumber. He said naught when the work was ended, but surveyed the great fragrant piles of cedar and walnut and maple and cherry and oak, the building woods of these richly endowed mountains, with a silence so significant that it spoke louder than words. It said that his work was finished, and who was there who would do as much or more? So loud, so forceful, so eloquent was this challenge that the next day several teamsters came and stood dismally each holding his chin-whiskers in his hand and contemplated the field of practical Christianity.

"It'll be a powerful job ter hev ter haul all that thar lumber, sure!" said one reluctant wight, in disconsolate survey, his mouth slightly ajar, his hand ruefully rubbing his cheek.

"It war a powerful job ter saw it," said the miller.

The jaws of the teamster closed with a snap. He had nothing more to say. He, too, was roused to the gospel of action. The miller should not saw more than he would haul. Thus it was that the next day found him with his strong mule team at sunrise, the first great lengths of the boles on the wagon, making his way along the steep ascents of Jolton's Ridge.

And again Mark looked on drearily. He could do naught—he and Cockleburr. Cockleburr was hardly broken to the saddle, wild and restive, and it would have been the sacrifice of a day's labor, even if the offer of such unlikely aid would have been accepted, to hitch the colt in for the hauling of this heavy lumber, such earnest, hearty work as the big mules were straining every muscle to accomplish. He was too poor, he felt, with a bitter sigh. He could do naught—naught. True, he armed himself with an axe, and went ahead of the toiling mules, now and then cutting down a sapling which grew in the midst of the unfrequented bridle-path, and which was not quite slight enough to bend beneath the wagon as did most of such obstructions, or widening the way where the clustering underbrush threatened a stoppage of the team. So much more, under the coercion of the little preacher's sermon, he had wanted to do, that he hardly cared for the "Holped me powerful, Mark," of the teamster's thanks, when they had reached the destination of the lumber—the secluded nook where the little mountain graveyard nestled in the heart of the great range—the site chosen by the neighbors for the erection of their beloved church. Beloved before one of the bowlders that made the piers of its foundation was selected from the rocky hillside, where the currents of forgotten, long ebbed-away torrents had stranded them, where the detrition of the rain and the sand had molded them, the powers of nature thus beginning the building of the church-house to the glory of God in times so long gone past that man has no record of its spaces. Beloved before one of the great logs was lifted upon another to build the walls, within which should be crystallized the worship of congregations, the prayers of the righteous that should avail much. Beloved before one of the puncheons was laid of the floor, consecrated with the hope that many a sinner should tread them on the way to salvation. Beloved with the pride of a worthy achievement and the satisfaction of a cherished duty honestly discharged, before a blow was struck or a nail driven.

And here Mark, earnestly seeking his

opportunity to share the work, found a field of usefulness. No great skill, one may be sure, prevailed in the methods of the humble handicraftsmen of the gorge—all untrained to the mechanical arts, and each a jack-of-all-trades, as occasion in his lowly needs or opportunity might offer. Mark had a sort of knack of deftness, a quick and exact eye, both suppleness and strength, and thus he was something more than a mere botch of an amateur workman. His enthusiasm blossomed forth. He, too, might serve the great cause. He, too, might give of the work of his hands.

At it he was, hammer and nails, from morning till night, and he rejoiced when the others living at a distance and having their firesides to provide for, left him here late alone building the temple of God in the wilderness. He would ever and anon glance out through the interstices of the unchinked log walls at the great sun going down over the valley behind the purple mountains of the west, and lending him an extra beam to drive another nail, after one might think it time to be dark and still; and vouchsafing yet another ray, as though loath to quit this work, lingering at the threshold of the day, although the splendors of another hemisphere awaited its illumination, and many a rich Southern scene that the sun is wont to love; and still sending a gleam, high aslant, that one more nail might be driven; and at last the red suffusion of certain farewell, wherein was enough light for the young man to catch up his tools and set out swiftly and joyously down the side of Jolton's Ridge.

And always was he first at the tryst to greet the sun—standing in the unfinished building, his hammer in his hand, his hat on the back of his head, and looking through the gap of the range to watch the great disk when it would rise over the Carolina Mountains, with its broad, prophetic effulgence falling over the lowly mounds in the graveyard, as if one might say, "Behold! the dispersal of night, the return of light, the earnest of the Day to come." Long before the other laborers on the church reached the building Mark had listened to the echoes keeping tally with the strokes of his hammer, had heard the earth shake, the clangor and clash of the distant train on the rails, the shriek of the whistle as the locomotive rushed upon the bridge above that deep chasm, the sinister hollow roar of the wheels, and the deep, thunderous reverberation of the rocks. Thus he noted the passage of the early trains—the freight first, and after an hour's interval the passenger train; then a silence, as if primeval, would settle down upon the world, broken only by the strokes of the hammer, until at last some neighbor, with his own tools in hand, would come in.

None of them realized how much of the work Mark had done. Each looked only at the result, knowing it to be the aggregated industry and leisure of the neighbors, laboring as best they might and as opportunity offered. This was no hindrance to Mark's satisfaction. He had wanted to help, not to make a parade of his help, or to have what he had done appreciated. He thought the little preacher, the "skimpy saint," as his unfriends called him, had a definite idea of what he had done. In the stress of this man's lofty ideals he could compromise with little that failed to reach them. He was forever stretching onward and upward. But Mark noted a kindling in his intent eye one day, while "the chinking" was being put in, the small diagonal slats between the logs of the wall on which the clay of the "daubing" was to be plastered. "Did you do all this side?" he had asked.

As Mark answered "Yes," he felt his heart swell with responsive pride to win even this infrequent look of approval, and he went on to claim more. "Don't tell nobody," he said, glancing up from his kneeling posture by the side of the wall. "But I done that corner, too, over thar by the door. Old Joel Ruggles done it fust, but the old man's eyesight's dim, an' his hand onstiddy, an' 'twar all crooked an' onreg'lar, so *unbeknown* ter *him* I kem hyar early one day an' did it over, —though he don't know it,—so ez 'twould be ekal—all of a piece."

The "skimpy saint" now hardly seemed to care to glance at the work. He still stood with his hand on the boy's shoulder, looking down at him with eyes in which Mark perceived new meanings.

"You can sense, then, the worth of hevin' all things of a piece with the best. See ter it, Mark, that ye keep yer life all of a piece with this good work—with the best that's in ye."

So Mark understood. But nowadays he hardly felt all of a piece with the good work he had done on the church walls, against so many discouragements, laboring early and late, seeking earnestly some means that might be within his limited power. Oftentimes, after the church was finished, he went and stood and gazed at it, realizing its stanch validity, without short-comings, without distortions—all substantial and regular, with none of the discrepancies

and inadequacies of his moral structure.

While silently and meditatively recalling all these facts as he sat this
night of early spring among the widely
unrelated surroundings of the still, the
shadowy group of moonshiners about
him, Mark Yates looked hard at Panther Brice's sharp features, showing, in
the thread of white light from the closed
door of the furnace, with startling dis-
tinctness against the darkness, like
some curiously carved cameo. He
never understood the rush of feeling
that constrained him to speak, and
afterward, when he thought of it, his
temerity surprised him.

"Painter," he said, "I hev been
a-comin' hyar ter this hyar still-house
along of ye an' the t'other boys right
smart time, an' I hev been mighty well
treated; an' I ain't one o' the sort ez
kin buy much liquor, nuther. I hev

hed a many a free drink hyar, an' a sight o' laughin' an' talkin' along o' ye an' the t'other boys. An' 'twarn't the whisky as brung me, nuther— 'twar mos'ly ter hear them yarns o' yourn 'bout bar-huntin' an' sech, fur ye air the talkin'est one o' the lot. But ef ye air a-goin' ter take it out'n the preacher or the church-house—I hain't got the rights o' what ye air a-layin' off ter do, an' I don't want ter know, nuther—jes' 'kase ye an' the t'other boys war turned out'n the church, I hev hed my fill o' associatin' with ye. I ain't a-goin' ter hev nuthin' ter do with men-folks ez would fight a pore critter of a preacher, what hev got ez much right ter jow ez ef he war a woman. Sass is what they both war made fur, it 'pears like ter me, an' 'twar toler'ble spunky sure in him ter speak his mind so plain, knowing what a fighter ye be an' the t'others, too—

no other men hev got the name of sech tremenjious fighters! I allow he seen his jewty plain in what he done, seein' he tuk sech risks. An' ef ye air a-goin' ter raise a 'sturbance ter the church-house, or whatever ye air a-layin' off ter do ter *it*, I ain't a-goin' ter hev no hand-shakin' with sech folks. Payin' 'em back ain't a-goin' ter patch up the matter nohow—ye're done turned out the church now, an' that ain't a-goin' ter put ye back. It 'pears mighty cur'ous ter me ez a man ez kin claw with a bar same ez with a little purp, kin git so riled ez he'll take up with fightin' of that thar pore little preacher what ain't got a ounce o' muscle ter save his life. I wouldn't mind his jowin' at me no more'n I mind my mother's jowin'—an' she air always at it."

There was a silence for a few moments—only the sound of the trickling liquor from the worm and the whir inside the still. That white face, illumined by the thread of light, was so motionless that it might have seemed petrified but for the intense green glare of the widely open eyes. The lips suddenly parted in a snarl, showing two rows of sharp white teeth, and the high shrill voice struck the air with a shiver.

"Ye're the cussedest purp in this hyar gorge!" the Panther exclaimed. "Ye sit thar an' tell how well ye hev been treated hyar ter this hyar still-house, an' then let on ez how ye think ye're too good ter come a-visitin' hyar any more. Ye air like all the rest o' these folks round hyar—ye take all ye wants, an' then the fust breath of a word agin a body ye turns agin 'em too. Ye kin clar out'n this. Ye ain't wanted hyar. I ain't a-goin' ter let none o' yer church brethren nor thar fr'en's nuther—fur ye ain't even a perfessin' member—come five mile a-nigh hyar arter this. We air a-goin' ter turn 'em out'n the still-house, an' that thar will hurt 'em worse'n turnin' 'em out'n the church. They go an' turn *us* out'n the church fur runnin' of a still, an' before the Lord, we kin hardly drive 'em away from hyar along of we-uns. I'm a-goin' ter git the skin o' one o' these hyar brethren an' nail it ter the door like a mink's skin ter a hen house, an' I'll see ef that can't skeer 'em off. An' ef ye don't git out'n hyar mighty quick now, Mark Yates, like ez not the fust skin nailed ter the door will be that thar big, loose hide o' yourn.''

''I ain't the man ter stay when I'm axed ter go,'' said young Yates, rising, ''an' so I'll light out right now. But what I war a-aimin' ter tell ye, Painter, war ez how I hev sot too much store by ye and the t'other boys ter want ter see ye a-cuttin' cur'ous shines 'bout the church-house an' that leetle mite of a preacher an' sech.''

Once more that mental reservation touching "the strength of righteousness" recurred to him. Was the little preacher altogether a weakling? His courage was a stanch endowment. He had been warned of the gathering antagonisms a hundred times, and by friend as well as foe. But obstinately, resolutely, he kept on the path he had chosen to tread.

"An' I'll let ye know ez I kin be frien'ly with a man ez fights bars an' fightin'-men," Mark resumed, "but I kin abide no man ez gits ter huntin' down little scraps of preachers what hain't got no call ter fight, nor no muscle nuther."

"Ye'll go away 'thout that thar hide o' yourn ef ye don't put out mighty quick now,'' said the Panther, his sinister green eyes ablaze and his supple body trembling with eagerness to leap upon his foe.

"I ain't afeard of ye, Painter," said Mark, with his impenetrable calm, "but this hyar still-house air yourn, an' I s'pose ez ye hev got a right ter say who air ter stay an' who air ter go."

He went out into the chill night; the moon had sunk; the fleet of clouds rode at anchor above the eastern horizon, and save the throbbing of the constellations the sky was still. But the strong, cold wind continued to circle close about the surface of the earth; the pines were swaying to and fro, and moaning as they swayed; the bare branches of the other trees crashed fitfully together. As Yates mounted his horse he heard Aaron say, in a fretful tone: "In the name of God,

John, what ails ye to-night? Ye tuk Mark an' Mose up ez sharp! Ye air ez powerful bouncin' ez ef ye hed been drunk fur a week.''

The keen voice of the Panther rang out shrilly, and Mark gave his horse whip and heel to be beyond the sound of it. He wanted to hear no more—not even the tones—least of all the words, and words spoken in confidence in their own circle when they believed themselves unheard. He feared there was some wicked conspiracy among them; he could not imagine what it might be, but since he could do naught to hinder he earnestly desired that he might not become accidentally cognizant of it, and in so far accessory to it. He therefore sought to give them some intimation of his lingering presence, for Cockleburr had been frisky and restive, and difficult to mount; he accordingly began to sing aloud:—

"You hear that hawn? Yo he! Yo ho!"

But what was this? Instead of his customary hearty whoop, the tones rang out all forlornly, a wheeze and a quaver, and finally broke and sunk into silence. But the voices in conversation within had suddenly ceased. The musically disposed of the Brice brothers himself was singing, as if quite casually:—

"He wept full sore fur his 'dear friend Jack,'
An' how could I know he meant 'Apple-Jack'!"

Mark was aware that they had taken his warning, although with no appreciation of his motive in giving it. He could imagine the contemptuous anger against him with which they looked significantly at one another as they sat in the dusky shadows around the still, and he knew that his sudden outburst into song must seem to them bravado—an intimation that he did not care for having been summarily ejected from the still-house, when in reality, only the recollection of it sent the color flaming to his cheeks and the tears to his eyes. This was not for the mere matter of pride, either; but for disappointment, for fled illusions, for the realization that he had placed a false valuation on these men. He had been flattered that they had cared for his friendship, and reciprocally had valued him more than others; they had relished and invited his companionship; they had treated him almost as one of themselves. And although he saw much gambling and drinking, sometimes resulting in brawls and furious fights, against which his moral sense revolted, he felt sure that their dissipation was transitory; they would all straighten out and settle down—when they themselves were older. In truth, he could hardly have conceived that this manifestation of to-night was the true identity of the friends to whom he had attached himself—that their souls, their hearts, their minds, were of a piece with the texture of their daily lives, as sooner or later the event would show. In the disuse of good impulses and honest qualities they grow lax and weak. They are the moral muscles of the spiritual being, and, like the muscles of the physical body, they must needs be exercised and trained to serve the best interests of the soul.

"Yo-he! Yo-ho!" sang poor Mark, as he plunged into the forest, keeping in the wood trail, called courteously a road, partly by the memory of his horse, and partly by the keen sight of his gray eyes. He lapsed presently into silence, for he had no heart for singing, and he jogged on dispirited, gloomy, reflective, through the rugged ways of the wilderness. It was fully two hours before he emerged into the more open country about his mother's house; as he reached the bank of the stream he glanced up, toward the bridge—the faintest suggestion of two parallel lines across the instarred sky. A great light flashed through the heavens, followed by a comet-like sweep of fiery sparks.

"That thar air the 'leven o'clock train, I reckon," said Mark, making his cautious way among the bowlders and fragments of fallen rock to the door of the house. The horse plucked up spirit to neigh gleefully at the sight of his shanty and the thought of his supper. The sound brought Mrs. Yates to the window of the cabin.

"Air that ye a-comin', Mark?" she asked.

"It air me an' Cockleburr," replied her son, with an effort to be cheerful too, and to cast away gloomy thoughts in the relief of being once more at home.

"Air ye ez drunk ez or'nary?" demanded his mother.

This was a damper. "I ain't drunk nohow in the worl'," said Mark, sullenly.

"Whyn't ye stay ter the still, then, till ye war soaked?" she gibed at him.

Mark dismounted in silence; there was no saddle to be unbuckled, and Cockleburr walked at once into the little shed to munch upon a handful of hay and to dream of corn.

His master, entering the house, was saluted by the inquiry, "War Painter Brice ez drunk ez common?"

"No, he warn't drunk nuther."

"Hev the still gone dry?" asked

Mrs. Yates, affecting an air of deep interest.

"Not ez I knows on, it hain't," said Mark.

"Thar must be suthin' mighty comical a-goin on ef ye nor Painter nare one air drunk. Is Aaron drunk, then? Nor Pete? nor Joe? Waal, this air powerful disapp'intin'." And she took off her spectacles, wiped them on her apron, and shook her head slowly to and fro in solemn mockery.

"Waal," she continued, with a more natural appearance of interest, "what war they all a-talkin' 'bout ter-night?"

Mark sat down, and looked gloomily at the dying embers in the deep chimney-place for a moment, then he replied, evasively, "Nuthin' much."

"That's what ye always say! Ef I go from hyar ter the spring yander, I kin come back with more to tell than yer kin gether up in a day an' a night at the still. It 'pears like ter me men war mos'ly made jes' ter eat an' drink, an' thar tongues war gin 'em for no use but jes' ter keep 'em from feelin' lonesome like.''

Mark did not respond to this sarcasm. His mother presently knelt down on the rough stones of the hearth, and began to rake the coals together, covering them with ashes, preliminary to retiring for the night. She glanced up into his face as she completed the work; then, with a gleam of fun in her eyes, she said:

"Ye look like ye're studyin' powerful hard, Mark. Mebbe ye air a-cornsiderin' 'bout gittin' married. It's 'bout time ez ye war a-gittin' another woman hyar ter work fur ye, 'kase I'm toler'ble old, an' can't live forever mo', an' some day ye'll find yerself desolated.''

"I ain't a-studyin' no more 'bout

a-gettin' married nor ye air yerself,''
Mark retorted, petulantly.

"Ye ain't a-studyin' much 'bout it,
then,'' said his mother. "The Bible
looks like it air a-pityin' of widders
mightily, but it 'pears ter me that the
worst of thar troubles is over.''

Then ensued a long silence. "Thar's
one thing to be sartain,'' said Mark,
suddenly. "I ain't never a-goin ter
that thar still no more.''

"I hev hearn ye say that afore,''
remarked Mrs. Yates, dryly. "An'
thar never come a day when yer father
war alive ez he didn't say that very
word—nor a day as that word warn't
bruken.''

These amenities were at length
sunk in sleep, and the little log
hut hung upon its precarious perch
on the slope beneath the huge cliff
all quiet and lonely. The great gorge
seemed a channel hewn for the winds;

they filled it with surging waves of sound, and the vast stretches of woods were in wild commotion. The Argus-eyed sky still held its steadfast watch, but an impenetrable black mask clung to the earth. At long intervals there arose from out the forest the cry of a wild beast—the anguish of the prey or the savage joy of the captor—and then for a time no sound save the monotonous ebb and flow of the sea of winds. Suddenly, a shrill whistle awoke the echoes, the meteor-like train sweeping across the sky wavered, faltered, and paused on the verge of the crag. Then the darkness was instarred with faint, swinging points of light, and there floated down upon the wind the sound of eager, excited voices.

"Ef them thar cars war ter drap off'n that thar bluff," said the anxious Mrs. Yates, as she and her son, aroused by the unwonted noise, came out of the hut, and gazed upward at the great white glare of the headlight, "they'd ruin the turnip patch, worl' without e-end."

"Nothing whatever is the matter," said the Pullman conductor, cheerily, to his passengers, as he re-entered his coach. "Only a little church on fire just beyond the curve of the road; the engineer couldn't determine at first whether it was a fire built on the track or on the hillside."

The curtains of the berths were dropped, sundry inquiring windows were closed, the travelers lay back on their hard pillows, the faint swinging points of light moved upward as the men with the lanterns sprang upon the platforms, the train moved slowly and majestically across the bridge, and presently it was whizzing past the little church, where the flames had licked up benches and pulpit and floor, and were beginning to stream through door and window, and far above the roof.

The miniature world went clanging along its way, careless of what it left behind, and the turnip patch was saved.

The wonderful phenomenon of the stoppage of the train had aroused the whole countryside, and when it had passed, the strange lurid glare high on the slope of the mountain attracted attention. There was an instant rush of the scattered settlers toward the doomed building. A narrow, circuitous path led them up the steep ascent among gigantic rocks and dense pine thickets; the roaring of the tumultuous wind drowned all other sounds, and they soon ceased the endeavor to speak to one another as they went, and canvass their suspicions and indignation. Turning a sharp curve, the foremost of the party came abruptly upon a man descending.

He had felt secure in the dead hour of night and the thick darkness, and the distance had precluded him from being warned by the stoppage of the train. He stood in motionless indecision for an instant, until Moses Carter, who was a little in advance of the others, made an effort to seize him, exclaiming, "This fire ez ye hev kindled, Painter Brice, will burn ye in hell forever!" He spoke at a venture, not recognizing the dark shadow, but there was no mistaking the supple spring with which the man threw himself upon his enemy, nor the keen ferocity that wielded the sharp knife. Hearing, however, in the ebb of the wind, voices approaching from the hill below, and realizing the number of his antagonists, the Panther tore himself loose, and running in the dark with the unerring instinct and precision of the wild beast that he was, he sped up the precipitous slope, and was lost in the gloomy night.

"Gin us the slip!" exclaimed Joel Ruggles, in grievous disappointment, as he came up breathless. "A cussed painter if ever thar war one."

"Mebbe he won't go fur," said Moses Carter. "He done cut my arm a-nigh in two, but thar air suthin' a-drippin' off 'n my knife what I feels in my bones is that thar Painter's blood. An' I ain't a-goin ter stop till he air cotched, dead or alive. He mought hev gone down yander ter the Widder Yates's house, ez him an' Mark air thicker'n thieves. Come ter think on't," he continued, "Mark war a-settin' with this hyar very Painter Brice an' the t'others yander ter the still-house nigh 'pon eight o'clock ter-night, an' like ez not he holped

Painter an' the t'others ter fire the church." For there was a strong impression prevalent that wherever Panther Brice was, his satellite brothers were not far off. Nothing, however, was seen of them on the way, and the pursuers burst in upon the frightened widow and her son with little ceremony. Her assertion that Mark had not left home since the eleven o'clock train passed was disregarded, and they dragged the young fellow out to the door, demanding to know where were the Brices.

"I hain't seen none of 'em since I lef' the still 'bout'n eight or nine o'clock ter-night," Mark protested.

"Ef the truth war knowed," said Moses Carter, jeeringly, "ye never lef' the still till they did. War it ye ez holped 'em ter fire the church?"

"I never knowed the church war burnin' till ye kem hyar," replied young Yates.   He was almost over-powered by a sickening realization of the meaning of those covert insinua-tions which he had heard at the still; and he remembered that the Panther's assertion that the church was safer with the Brices in it than out of it, was made while he sat among the brothers in Moses Carter's presence. He saw the justice of the strong sus-picion.

"You know, though, whar Painter Brice is now—don't ye?" asked Carter.

A faint streak of dawn was athwart the eastern clouds, and as the young fellow turned his bewildered eyes upward to it the blood stood still in his veins.   Upon one of the parallel lines of the bridge was the figure of man, belittled by the distance, and indis-tinctly defined against the mottling sky; but the far-seeing gray eyes detected in a certain untrammeled ease, as it moved lightly from one of the ties to another, the Panther's free motion.

Mark Yates hesitated. He cherished an almost superstitious reverence for the church which Panther Brice had desecrated and destroyed, and he feared the consequences of refusing to give the information demanded of him. A denial of the knowledge he did not for a moment contemplate. And struggling in his mind against these considerations was a recollection of the hospitality of the Brices, and of the ill-starred friendship that had taken root and grown and flourished at the still.

This hesitation was observed; there were significant looks interchanged among the men, and the question was repeated, "Whar's Painter Brice?"

The decision of the problems that agitated the mind of Mark Yates was not left to him. He saw the figure on the bridge suddenly turn, then start eagerly forward. A heavy freight train, almost noiseless in the wild whirl of the wind, had approached very near without being perceived by Panther Brice. He could not retrace his way before it would be upon him —to cross the bridge in advance of it was his only hope. He was dizzy from the loss of blood and the great height, and the wind was blowing between the cliffs in a strong, unobstructed current. As he ran rapidly onward, the first faint gleam of the approaching headlight touched the bridge—a furious warning shriek of the whistle mingled with a wild human cry, and the Panther, missing his footing, fell like a thunderbolt into the depths of the black waters below.

There was a revulsion of feeling, very characteristic of inconstant humanity, in the little group on the slope below the crag. Before Mark Yates's frantic exclamation, "Thar goes Painter Brice, an' he'll be drownded sure!" had fairly died upon the air, half a dozen men were struggling in the dark, cold water of the swift stream in the vain attempt to rescue their hunted foe. Long after they had given up the forlorn hope of saving his life, the morning sun for hours watched them patrolling the banks for the recovery of the body.

"Ef we could haul that pore critter out somehow 'nother," said Moses Carter, his arm still dripping from the sharp strokes of the Panther's knife, "an' git the preacher ter bury him somewhar under the pines like he war a Christian, I could rest more sati'fied in my mind."

The mountain stream never gave him up.

This event had a radical influence

upon the future of Mark Yates. Never again did he belittle the possible impetus given the moral nature by those more trifling wrongs that always result in an increased momentum toward crime. He was the first to discover more of what Painter Brice had really intended,—had attempted,—than was immediately apparent to the countryside in general. A fragment of the door lay unburned among the charred remains of the little church in the wilderness—a fragment that carried the lock, the key. Mark's sharp eyes fixed upon a salient point as he stood among the group that had congregated there in the sad light of the awakening day. The key was on the outside of the door, and it had been turned! The Panther had doubtless been actuated by revenge, and perhaps, had been influenced by the fear that information of the illicit distilling would be given by the parson to the revenue authorities, as a means of breaking up an element so inimical to the true progress of religion on the ridge—its denizens hitherto availing themselves of the convenience of the still to assuage any pricks of conscience they may have had in the matter, and also fearing the swift and terrible fate that inevitably overtook the informer. At all events, it was evident, that having reason to believe the minister was still within, Painter Brice had noiselessly locked the door that his unsuspecting enemy might also perish in the flames. For in the primitive fashioning of the building there was no aperture for light and air except the door—no window, save a small, glassless square above the pulpit which, in the good time coming, the congregation had hoped to glaze, to receive therefrom more light on salvation. It was so small, so high, that perhaps no other man could have slipped through it, save indeed the slim little "skimpy saint," and it was thus that he had escaped.

No vengeance followed the Panther's brothers. "They hed ter do jes' what Painter tole 'em, ye see," was the explanation of this leniency. And Mark Yates was always afterward described as "a peart smart boy, ef he hedn't holped the Brices ter fire the church-house." The still continued to be run according to the old regulations, except there was no whisky sold to the church brethren. "That bein' the word ez John left behind him," said Aaron. The laws of few departed rulers are observed with the rigor which the Brices accorded to the Panther's word. The locality came to be generally avoided, and no one cared to linger there after dark, save the three

Brices, who sat as of old, in the black shadows about the still.

Whenever in the night-wrapped gorge a shrill cry is heard from the woods, or the wind strikes a piercing key, or the train thunders over the bridge with a wild shriek of whistles, and the rocks repeat it with a human tone in the echo, the simple foresters are wont to turn a trifle pale and to bar up the doors, declaring that the sound "air Painter Brice a-callin' fur his brothers."

THE EXPLOIT
OF
CHOOLAH, THE CHICKASAW

THE EXPLOIT

OF

CHOOLAH, THE CHICKASAW

The victorious campaign which Lieutenant-Colonel James Grant conducted in the Cherokee country in the summer of 1761, and which redounded so greatly to the credit of the courage and endurance of the expeditionary force, British regulars and South Carolina provincials, is like many other human events in presenting to the casual observation only an harmonious whole, while it is made up of a thousand little jagged bits of varied incident inconsistent and irregular, and with no single element in common but the attraction of cohesion to amalgamate the mosaic.

217

CHOOLAH, THE CHICKASAW

Perhaps no two men in the command saw alike the peaks of the Great Smoky Mountains hovering elusively on the horizon, now purple and ominous among the storm clouds, for the rain fell persistently; now distant, blue, transiently sun-flooded, and with the prismatic splendors of the rainbow spanning in successive arches the abysses from dome to dome, and growing ever fainter and fainter in duplication far away. Perhaps no two men revived similar impressions as they recognized various localities from the South Carolina coast to the Indian town of Etchoee, near the Little Tennessee River, for many of them had traversed hundreds of miles of these wild fastnesses the previous year, when Colonel Montgomery, now returned to England, had led an aggressive expedition against the Cherokees. Certain it is, the accounts of their experiences are many and varied—only in all the character of their terrible enemy, the powerful and warlike Cherokee, stands out as incontrovertible as eternity, as immutable as Fate. Hence there were no stragglers, no deserters. In a compact body, while the rain fell, and the torrents swelled the streams till the fords became almost impracticable, the little army, as with a single impulse, pressed stanchly on through the mist-filled, sodden avenues of the primeval woods. To be out of sight for an instant of that long, thin column of soldiers risked far more than death — capture, torture, the flame, the knife, all the extremity of anguish that the ingenuity of savage malice could devise and human flesh endure. But although day by day the thunder cracked among the branches of the dripping trees and reverberated from the rocks of the craggy defiles, and keen swift blades of lightning at short intervals thrust through the lowering clouds, almost always near sunset long level lines of burnished golden beams began to glance through the wild woodland ways; a mocking-bird would burst into song from out the dense coverts of the laurel on the slope of a mountain hard by; the sky would show blue overhead, and glimmer red through the low-hanging boughs toward the west; and the troops would pitch their tents under the restored peace of the elements and the placid white stars.

A jolly camp it must have been. Stories of it have come down to this day — of its songs, loud, hilarious, patriotic, doubtless rudely musical; of its wild pranks, of that boyish and jocose kind denominated by sober and unsympathetic elders, "horse-play"; of the intense delight experienced by

CHOOLAH, THE CHICKASAW

the savage allies, the Chickasaws, who
participated in the campaign, in wit-
nessing the dances of the young Highlanders—how "their sprightly manner
in this exercise," and athletic grace
appealed to the Indians; how the
sound of the bag-pipes thrilled them;
how they admired that ancient martial
garb, the kilt and plaid.

No admiration, however extravagant of Scotch customs, character, or
appearance, seemed excessive in the
eyes of Lieutenant-Colonel James
Grant, so readily did his haughty,
patriotic pride acquiesce in it, and
the Indian's evident appreciation of
the national superiority of the Scotch
to all other races of men duly served
to enhance his opinion of the mental
acumen of the Chickasaws. This
homage, however, failed to mollify or
modify the estimate of the noble red-
man already formed by a certain sub-

altern, Lieutenant Ronald MacDonnell.

"The Lord made him an Indian—
and an Indian he will remain," he
would remark sagely.

The policy of the British govern-
ment to utilize in its armies the martial
strength of semi-savage dependencies,
elsewhere so conspicuously exploited,
was never successful with these Indians
save as the tribes might fight in
predatory bands in their own wild
way, although much effort was made
looking toward regular enlistments.
And, in fact, the futility of all en-
deavors to reduce the savage to a
reasonable conformity to the milita-
rism of the camp, to inculcate the
details of the drill, a sense of the
authority of officers, the obliga-
tions of out-posts, the heinousness of
"running the guard," the necessity
of submitting to the prescribed punish-

ments and penalties for disobedience of orders,—all rendered this ethnographic saw so marvelously apt, that it seemed endowed with more wisdom than Ronald MacDonnell was popularly supposed to possess. But such logic as he could muster operated within contracted limits. If the Lord had not fitted a man to be a soldier, why — there Ronald MacDonnell's extremest flights of speculation paused.

In the scheme of his narrow-minded Cosmos the human creature was represented by two simple species: unimportant, unindividualized man in general, and that race of exalted beings known as soldiers. He was a good drill, and with the instinct of a born disciplinarian in his survey, he would often watch the Chickasaws with this question in his mind,—sometimes when they were on the march, and their endurance, their activity, the admirable proportions of their bodies, their free and vigorous gait were in evidence; sometimes in the swift efficiency of their scouting parties when their strategy and courage and wily caution were most marked; sometimes in the relaxations of the camp when their keen responsive interest in the quirks and quips of the soldier at play attested their mental receptivity and plastic impressibility. Their gayety seemed a docile, mundane, civilized sort of mirth when they would stand around in the ring with the other soldiers to watch the agile Highlanders in the inspiring martial posturing of the sword dance, with their fluttering kilts and glittering blades, their free gestures, their long, sinewy, bounding steps, as of creatures of no weight, while the bag-pipes skirled, and the great campfire flared, and the light and shadows fluctuated in the dense prime-

val woods, half revealing, half concealing the lines of tents, of picketed horses,
of stacks of arms, of other flaring
camp-fires—even the pastoral suggestion in the distance of the horned
heads of the beef-herd. But whatever the place or scene, Ronald Mac-
Donnell's conclusion was essentially
the same. "The Lord made him an
Indian," he would say, with an air
of absolute finality.

He was a man of few words,—
of few ideas; these were strictly
military and of an appreciated
value. He was considered a promising
young officer, and was often detailed to
important and hazardous duty. And
if he had naught to say at mess, and
seldom could perceive a joke unless
of a phenomenal pertinence and brilliancy, broadly aflare so to speak under
his nose, he was yet a boon companion, and could hold his own like a

Scotchman when many a brighter man was under the table. He had a certain stanch, unquestioning sense of duty and loyalty, and manifested an unchangeable partisanship in his friendship, of a silent and undemonstrative order, that caused his somewhat exaggerated view of his own dignity to be respected, for it was intuitively felt that his personal antagonism would be of the same tenacious, unreasoning, requiting quality, and should not be needlessly roused. He was still very young, although he had seen much service. He was tall and stalwart; he had the large, raw-boned look which is usually considered characteristic of the Scotch build, and was of great muscular strength, but carrying not one ounce of superfluous flesh. Light-colored ·hair, almost flaxen, indeed, with a strong tendency to curl in the shorter locks that lay in tendrils on his

CHOOLAH, THE CHICKASAW

forehead, clear, contemplative blue eyes, a fixed look of strength, of reserves of unfailing firmness about the well-cut lips, a good brick-red flush acquired from many and many a day of marching in the wind, and the rain, and the sun—this is the impression one may take from his portrait. He could be as noisy and boisterously gay as the other young officers, but somehow his hilarity was of a physical sort, as of the sheer joy of living, and moving, and being so strong. One might wonder what impressions he received in the long term of his service in Canada and the Colonies — these strange new lands so alien to all his earlier experience. One might doubt if he saw how fair of face was this most lovely of regions, the Cherokee country; if the primeval forests, the splendid tangles of blooming rhododendron, the crystal-clear, rock-bound rivers were asserted in his consciousness other-wise than as the technical " obstacle" for troops on the march. As to the imposing muster of limitless ranks of mountains surrounding the little army on every side, they did not remind him of the hills of Scotland, as the sheer sense of great heights and wild ravines and flashing cataracts sug-gested reminiscences to the others. "There is no gorse," he remarked of these august ranges, with their rich growths of gigantic forest trees, as if from the beginning of the earliest eras of dry land,—and the mess called him "Gorse" until the incident was for-gotten.

For the last three days the com-mand, consisting of some twenty-six hundred men, had been advancing by forced marches, despite the deterrent weather. Setting out on the 7th of June from Fort Prince George, where the army had rested for ten days after the march of three hundred miles from Charlestown, Colonel Grant encountered a season of phenomenal rain-fall. Moreover, the lay of the land,—long stretches of broken, rocky country, gashed by steep ravines and intersected by foaming, swollen torrents, deep and dangerous to ford, encompassed on every hand by rugged heights and narrow, intricate, winding valleys, affording always but a restricted passage,— offered peculiar advantages for attack. Colonel Grant, aware that these craggy defiles could be held against him even by an inferior force, that a smart demonstration on the flank would so separate the thin line of his troops that one division would hardly be available to come to the support of the other, that an engagement here and now would result in great loss of life, if not an actual and decisive repulse, was urging the march forward at the utmost speed possible to reach more practicable ground for an encounter, regardless how the pace might harass the men. But they were responding gallantly to the demands on their strength, and this was what he had hardly dared to hope. For during the previous winter, when General Amherst ordered the British regulars south by sea, many of them immediately upon their arrival in Charlestown, succumbed to an illness occasioned by drinking the brackish water of certain wells of the city. Coming in response to the urgent appeals of the province to the commander-in-chief of the army to defend the frontier against the turbulent Cherokees who ravaged the borders, the British force were looked upon as public deliverers, and the people of the city took the ill soldiers from the camps into their own private dwellings, nursing them until they were quite restored. No troops could have better endured the extreme hardships which they successfully encountered in their march northward. So swift an advance seemed almost impossible. The speed of the movement apparently had not been anticipated, even by that wily and watchful enemy, the Cherokees. It has been said that at this critical juncture the Indians had failed to receive the supply of ammunition from the French which they had anticipated, although a quantity, inadequate for the emergency, however, reached them a few days later. At all events Colonel Grant was nearly free of the district where disaster so menaced him before he received a single shot. He had profited much by his several campaigns in this country since he led that rash, impetuous, and bloody demonstration against Fort Duquesne, in which he himself was captured with nineteen of his officers, and his command was almost cut to pieces. Now his scouts patrolled the woods in every direction. His vanguard of Indian allies under command of a British officer was supported by a body of fifty rangers and one hundred and fifty light infantry. Every precaution against surprise was taken.

Late one afternoon, however, the main body wavered with a sudden shock. The news came along the line. The Cherokees were upon them— upon the flank? No; in force fiercely assaulting the rear-guard. It was as Grant had feared impossible in these narrow defiles to avail himself of his strength, to face about, to form, to give battle. The advance was ordered to continue steadily onward,—difficult indeed, with the sound of the musketry and shouting from the rear, now louder, now fainter, as the surges of attack ebbed and flowed.

A strong party was detached to reinforce the rear-guard. But again and again the Cherokees made a spirited dash, seeking to cut off the beef herd, fighting almost in the open, with as definite and logical a military plan of destroying the army by capturing its supplies in that wild country, hundreds of miles from adequate succor, as if devised by men trained in all the theories of war.

"The Lord made him—" muttered Ronald MacDonnell, in uncertainty, recognizing the coherence of this military maneuver, and said no more. Whether or not his theory was reduced to that simple incontrovertible proposition, thus modified by the soldier-like demonstration on the supply train, his cogitations were cut short by more familiar ideas, when in command of thirty-two picked men, he was ordered to make a detour through the defiles of a narrow adjacent ravine, and, issuing suddenly thence, seek to fall upon the flank of the enemy and surprise, rout, and pursue him. This was the kind of thing, that with all his limitations, Ronald MacDonnell most definitely understood. This set a-quiver, with keenest sensitiveness, every fiber of his phlegmatic nature, called out every working capacity of his slow, substantial brains, made his quiet pulses bound. He looked the men over strictly as they dressed their ranks, and then he stepped swiftly forward toward them, for it was the habit to speak a few words of encouragement to the troops about to enter on any extra-hazardous duty, so daunting seemed the very sight of the Cherokees and the sound of their blood-curdling whoops.

CHOOLAH, THE CHICKASAW

"Hech, callants!" he cried, in his simple joy; and so full of valiant elation was the exclamation that its spirit flared up amongst the wild "petticoat-men," who cheered as lustily as if they had profited by the best of logic and the most finely flavored eloquence. Ronald MacDonnell felt that he had acquitted himself well in the usual way, and was under the impression that he had made a speech to the troops.

Now climbing the crags of the verges of the ravine, now deep in its trough, following the banks of its flashing torrent, they made their way—at a brisk double-quick when the ground would admit of such progress—and when they must, painfully dragging one another through the dense jungles of the dripping laurel, always holding well together, remembering the ever-frightful menace of the Cherokee to the laggard. The rain fell no longer; the sunlight slanted on the summit of the rocks above their heads; the wind was blowing fresh and free, and the mists scurried before it; now and again on the steep slopes as the vapors shifted, the horned heads of cattle showed with a familiar reminiscent effect as of mountain kyloes at home. But these were great stall-fed steers, running furiously at large, bellowing, frightened by the tumults of the conflict, plunging along the narrow defiles, almost dashing headlong into the little party of Highlanders who were now quickening their pace, for the crack of dropping shots and once and again a volley, the whoopings of the savages and shouts of the soldiers, betokened that the scene of carnage was near.

Only a few of the cattle were astray for, as MacDonnell and his men emerged into a little level glade, they could see in the distance that the herd was held well together by the cattle-guard, while the reinforcements sought to check the Cherokees, who, although continually sending forth their terribly accurate masked fire from behind trees and rocks, now and again with a mounted body struck out boldly for the supply train, assaulting with tremendous impetuosity the rear-guard. So still and clear was the evening air that, despite the clamors of battle, MacDonnell could hear the commands, could see in the distance the lines rallying on the reserve forming into solid masses, as the mounted savages hurled down upon them; could even discern where rallies by platoon had been earlier made judging from the position of the bodies of the dead soldiers, lying in a half-suggested circle.

The next moment, with a ringing shout and a smartly delivered volley of · musketry the Highlanders flung themselves from out the mouth of the ravine. The Cherokee horsemen were going down like so many ten-pins. The first detachment of reinforcements set up a wild shout of joy to perceive the support, then flung themselves on their knees to load while a second volley from the Highlanders passed over their heads. The rearguard had formed anew, faced about, and were advancing in the opposite direction. The Cherokee horsemen, almost surrounded, gave way; the fire of the others in ambush wavered, slackened, became only a dropping shot here and there, then sunk to silence. And the woods were filled with a wild rout, with the irregular musketry of the troops frenzied with sudden success, out of line, out of hearing, out of reason as they pursued the unmounted savages, dislodged at last from their masked position; with the bugles blowing, the bag-pipes playing; with the unheard, disregarded orders shouted by the officers; with that thrilling cry of the Highlanders "Claymore! Claymore!" the sun flashing on their drawn broadswords as they gained on the flying Indians, themselves as fleet;—a confused, disordered panorama of shadows and sunlight, of men in red coats and men in blue, and men in tartan, and savage Chickasaws and Cherokees in their wild barbaric array.

It had been desired that the repulse should be fierce and decisive, the pursuit bloody and relentless. The supply train represented the life of the army, and it was essential to deter the Cherokees from readily renewing the attack on so vital a point. But these ends compassed, every effort of the officers was concentrated on the necessity of recalling the scattered parties. Night was coming on; it was a strange and an alien country; the skulking Cherokees were doubtless in force somewhere in the dense coverts of the woods, and the vicarious terrors of the capture that menaced the valorous and venturesome soldiers began to press heavily upon the officers. Again and again the bugles summoned the stragglers, the rich golden notes drifting through the wilderness, rousing a thousand insistent echoes from many a dumb rock thus endowed with a voice. Certain of the more solicitous officers sent out, with much caution, small details, gathering together the stragglers as they went.

How Ronald MacDonnell became separated from one of these parties was never very clear afterward to his own mind. His attention was attracted first by the sight of a canny Scotch face or two, which he knew, lying very low and very still; he suffered a pang which he could never evade. These were the men who had followed him to the finish, and he took out his note-book and holding it against a tree, made a memorandum of the locality for the burial parties, and then, with great particularity, of the names, "For the auld folks at hame," and he quoted, mournfully a line of the old Gaelic lament much sung by the Scotch emigrants "*Ha til mi tulidh*" (we return no more), which was sadly true of the Highland soldiery in the British ranks, —an instance is given of a regiment of twelve hundred men who served in America of whom only seventy-six ever saw their native hills again. Then, briskly putting up the book he went on a bit, glancing sharply about for the living of his command, even now thrusting their reckless heads into the den of the Cherokee lion. "Ill-fau'rd chields, and serve them right," he said, struggling with the dismay in his heart for their sake.

Perhaps he did not realize how far those active strides were carrying him from the command. In fact the march continued that night until the sinking of the moon, the army pressing resolutely on through the broken region of the mountain defiles. MacDonnell noted no Cherokee in sight, that is to say, not a living one. Several of the dead lay on the ground, their still faces already bearing that wan, listening, attentive look of death; they were heedless indeed of the hands that had rifled them of their possessions, for there were a few of the Chickasaw allies intent on plunder.

Presently as he went down a sunset glade, MacDonnell saw advancing a notable figure, a Chickasaw chief, tall, lithe, active, muscular, with a gait of athletic grace. He was wearing the warrior's "crown," a towering head-dress in the form of a circlet of white swan's feathers of graduated height, standing fifteen inches high in front, and at the bottom woven into a band of swan's down—all so deftly constructed that the method of the manufacture of the whole could not be discerned, it is said, without taking it into the hand. To the fringed borders of a sort of sleeveless hunting shirt of otter-skin and his buckskin leggings bits of shells were attached and glittered, and this betokened his wealth, for these beads represented the money of the Indians, with the unique advantage that when not in active circulation, one's currency could be worn as an ornament. It has been generally known under the generic name "wampum," although several of the Southern tribes called it "roanoke" or "pe-ack." It was made in tiny, tubular beads, of about an inch in length, of the conch and mussel-shells, requiring the illimitable leisure of the Indian to polish the cylinder to the desired glister, and drill through it the hollow no larger than a knitting-needle might fill. His chest and arms were painted symbolically in red and blue arabesques, and his face, of a proud, alert cast was smeared with vermilion and white. All his flesh glistened and shone with the polishing of some unguent. MacDonnell had heard a deal of preaching in his time of the Scotch Presbyterian persuasion, and in the dearth of expression Biblical phrases sometimes came to him. "Oil to give him a cheerful countenance," he quoted, still gazing at the grim face and figure. So intently he gazed, indeed, that the Indian hesitated, doubting if the Highland officer recognized him as a friend. Breaking off a branch of a green locust hard by and holding it aloft at one side, after the manner of a peaceful embassy, he continued his stately advance until within a yard of the silent Scotchman, also advancing. Then they both paused.

"*Ish la chu, Angona?*" said the Indian, in a sonorous voice. (Are you come, a friend?)

With the true Briton's aversion to palaver, intensified by his own incapacity for its practice, Ronald MacDonnell discovered little affinity for barbaric ceremonial. Nevertheless he was constrained by the punctilious sense that a gentleman must reply to a courteous greeting in the manner expected of him. His experience with the Chickasaws had acquainted him with the appropriate response.

"*Arabre—O, Angona,*" (I am come, a friend) he returned, a trifle sheepishly, and without the *ore rotundo* effect of the elocution of the Indian.

The young chief looked hard at him, evidently desirous of engaging him in conversation, unaware that it was a game at which the Scotchman was incapacitated for playing.

"Big battle," he observed, after a doubtful interval.

"A bonny ploy," assented the officer, who had seen much bigger ones.

Then they both paused and gazed at each other.

"Cherokee—heap fight! Big damn —O!" remarked Choolah, the Fox, applausively.

The use of this most vocative vowel as an intensive suffix is one of the peculiar methods of emphasis in the animated Chickasaw language—for instance the word *Yanas-O* means the biggest kind of buffalo (*yanasa* signifying buffalo in all the dialects). Choolah conversing in the cold and phlegmatic English evidently felt the need of these intensitives, and although a certain strong condemnatory monosyllable has been usually found sufficiently satisfying to the feelings of English speaking men seeking an expletive, the poor Aboriginal, wishing to be more wicked than he was, discovered its capacity for expansion with the prefix "Big" and devised an added emphasis with the explosive final "O."

"The Cherokee warriors? Pretty men!" said MacDonnell laconically, according the enemy's valor the meed of a soldier's praise. "Very pretty men."

Choolah had never piqued himself on his command of the English language, but he thought now his fluency was at least equal to that of this Scotchman, who really seemed to speak no tongue at all. As to the French—of that speech, *ookproo-se* (forever despised) Choolah would not learn a syllable, so deadly a hatred did the Chickasaw tribe bear the whole Gallic nation, dating back indeed through many wars and feuds, to the massacre by Choctaws of certain of the tribe in 1704, while under the protection of Boisbriant with a French safeguard, the deed suspected to have been committed if not at the instigation, at least by the permission of the French commander who, however, himself wounded in the affray, was beyond doubt, helpless in the matter.

"Heap tired?" ventured Choolah, at last, pining for conversation, his searching eyes on the young Highlander's face.

Ronald MacDonnell laughed a proud

negation. He held out one of his long, heavily muscled arms, with the fist clenched, that the Indian might feel, through his sleeve, the swelling cords that betokened his strength.

But it was Choolah's trait to cherish vanity in physical endowment, not to foster it in others. He only said, "Good! Swim river."

"Why swim the river?" demanded the Lieutenant.

Then Choolah detailed that through a scout he had thrown out he had learned that Colonel Grant's force, still pushing on, had succeeded in crossing the Tennessee river, the herd of cattle and the pack animals giving incredible trouble in the fords, deeply swollen by the unprecedented rains. It suddenly occurred to MacDonnell that, in view of the passage of the troops beyond this barrier, much caution would be requisite in endeavoring to rejoin the main body, lest they fall into the clutch of the Cherokees on the hither side, who doubtless would seek the capture of parties of stragglers by carefully patrolling the banks. He suggested this to Choolah. The Indian listened for only a moment with a look of deep conviction; then suddenly calling to five Chickasaws who were still engaged in parceling out the booty they had brought away from the dead bodies, he beckoned to MacDonnell, and they set out on a line parallel with the river, in Indian file, in a long, steady trot, the Scotchman among them, half willing, half dismayed, repudiating with the distaste of a prosaic, unimaginative mind every evidence of barbarism; every unaccustomed thing seemed grotesque and uncouth, and lacking all in lacking the cachet of civilization. Each man, as he ran lightly along that marshy turf, almost without noting, as if by instinct placed his feet upon the steps of the man in advance; thus, although seven persons passed over the ground, the largest man coming last, the footprints would show as if but one had gone that way. Ronald MacDonnell, quick at all military or athletic exercises, readily achieved conformity, although the barbarous procedure compromised his sensitive dignity, and he growled between his teeth something about a commissioned officer and a "demented goose-step," as if he found the practice of the one by the other a painful derogation. The moon came into the sky while still they sped along in this silent, crafty way, the wind in their faces, the pervasive scents of the damp, flowery June night filling every breath they drew with the impalpable essences of sylvan fragrance.

CHOOLAH, THE CHICKASAW

Even with the dangers that lurked at their heels, the Indians would never leap over a log, for this was unlucky, but made long detours around fallen trees, till Ronald MacDonnell could have belabored them with hearty good-will, and but for the fear of capture by the savage Cherokees, could not have restrained himself from crying aloud for rage for the waste of precious time. He had even less patience with their slow and respectful avoidance of stepping on a snake sinuously skirting their way, since, according to their belief, this would provoke the destruction of their own kindred by the serpent's brothers; Choolah's warning to the other Chickasaws in the half-suppressed hiss—"*Scente! Seente!*" (snake!) sounded far and sibilant in the quiet twilight. The Cherokee tribe also were wont to avoid with great heed any injury to snakes, and spoke of them always in terms of crafty compliment as "the bright old inhabitants."

The shadows grew darker, more definite; the moon, of a whiter glister now, thoughtful, passive, very melancholy, illumined the long vistas of the woods, and although verging toward the west, limited the area of darkness that had become their protection. More than once Choolah had glanced up doubtfully at its clear effulgence, for the sky was unclouded and the constellations were only a vague bespanglement of the blue deeps; coming at length to a dense covert among the blooming laurel, he crept in among the boughs, that overhung a shallow grotto by the river bank. MacDonnell followed his example, and the group soon were in the cleft of the rocks under the dense shade, the Scotchman alone among the Indians, with such dubious sentiments as a good hound might entertain were he thrust, muzzled, among his natural enemies, the bears.

But the Chickasaws, as ever, were earnestly, ardently friendly to the British. There was no surly reservation in Choolah's mind as he reached forth his hand and laid it upon the muscular arm of the Scotchman.

"Good arm," he said, reverting to the young Highlander's boast. "But—big damn—O!—good leg! Heap run!" he declared, with a smothered laugh, like any other young man's, much resembling indeed the affectionate ridicule that was wont to go around the mess-table at Ronald's unimaginative solemnities. But even MacDonnell could appreciate the jest at a brave man's activities, and he laughed in pleasant accord with the others.

A scout that they had thrown out came presently creeping back under the boughs with the unwelcome intelligence that there was a party of Cherokees a little higher up on the river, a small band of about a dozen men, seeming intent on holding the ford. These were stationary, apparently, but lower down, patrolling the banks, were groups here and there beating the woods for stragglers, he fancied. As yet, however, he thought they had no prisoners. Still, their suspicions of hidden soldiers were unallayed, and they were keeping very quiet.

The scout was named Oop-pa, the Owl. Although himself a warrior of note he was of a far lower grade of Chickasaw than Choolah, in personal quality as well as in actual rank. Instead of manifesting the stanch courage with which the Indian Fox hearkened to this untoward intelligence, the alert gathering of all his forces of mind and body for defense and for victory, or to make his defeat and capture an exceedingly costly and bloody triumph, Oop-pa set himself, still in the guise of imparting news, to sullenly plaining. The Highland officer listened heedfully for in these repeated campaigns in the valley of the Tennessee River he had become somewhat familiar with the dialect of the Chickasaw allies and in a degree they comprehended the sound of the English, and thus the conversation of the little party was chiefly held each speaking in his own tongue. The English were all across the river, Oop-pa declared. The red-coats, and the green-coats, and the tartan-men, and the provincial regiment—he did not believe a man of the command was left—but them.

"Well, thank God for that much grace!" exclaimed Ronald MacDonnell, strictly limiting his gratitude; he would render to Providence due recognition for his own rescue when it should be accomplished. His thankfulness, however, for the extent of the blessing vouchsafed was very genuine. His military conscience had been sharply pricked lest he might have lost some of his own men in the confusion of the pursuit and the subsequent separation from the little band.

Oop-pa looked at him surlily. For his own part, the Indian said, he was tired. Let the English and French fight one another. They had left him to be captured by the Cherokees. He needed no words. White man hated red man. Big Colonel Grant would be glad. Proud Colonel Grant—much prouder than an Indian,—would not care if the terrible Cherokees tortured and burned his faithful Chickasaws. Let it be one of his own honey plaidsmen, though, and you would see a difference! For haughty Colonel Grant couldn't abide for such little accidents to befall any of his pampered tartan-men, whom he loved as if they were his children.

With the word the world changed suddenly to Ronald MacDonnell. For this—this fearful fate menaced him. His was not a pictorial mind, but he had a sudden vision of a quiet house on a wild Scottish coast at nightfall within view of the surging Atlantic, with all the decorous habitudes about it of a kindly old home, with a window aglow, through which he could see, as if he stood just outside, a familiar room where there were old books and candlelight, and the flare of fire, and the collie on the rug, and the soft young pink cheeks of sisters, and a gray head with a pipe, intent upon the columns of a newspaper and the last intelligence from far America,—and oh! in the ingle-nook, a face sweeter for many a wrinkle, and eyes dearer for the loss of blue beauty, and soft hands grown nerveless, whose touch nevertheless he could feel across the ocean on his hard, weather-beaten young cheek. It had been a long time since this manly spirit had cried back to his mother, but it was only for a moment. If his fate came as he feared, he hoped they might never know how it had befallen. And the picture dissolved.

He did not fail to listen to the scornful reproaches with which Choolah upbraided Oop-pa. He had been left because he had lingered to rob the slain Cherokees. Look at the load there of hunting-shirts and blankets, and yes, even a plaid or two from a dead Highlander, that he had borne with him on his back from the field of battle; it was his avarice that had belated him.

And what then, Oop-pa retorted, had belated Choolah and the Highland officer? They had brought away nothing but their own hides, which they were at liberty to offer to the Cherokees, as early as they might.

The freedom of Oop-pa's tongue was resented as evidently by Choolah as by Ronald, but the *Etissu* occupied a semi-sacerdotal position toward the chief, a war-captain, the decrees of whose religion would not suffer him to touch a morsel of food or a drop of drink while on the war-path unless administered by the *Etissu*. The utmost abstemiousness was preserved among the Chickasaws throughout, and it continued a marvel to the British troops how men could march or fight so ill-nourished, practicing all the fasting austerities of religious observances. There were many similar customs implying consecration to war as holy duty, but they were gradually becoming modified by the introduction of foreign influences, for formerly the Indians would not have suffered among them on the march the unsanctified presence of a stranger like Ronald MacDonnell. He said naught in reply to the *Etissu*. His mind was grimly pre-occupied. He was busied with the realization of how strong he was, how very strong. These lithe Indians, with all their supple elasticity, their activity, had no such staying power as he, no such muscular vitality. He was thinking what resources of anguish his stalwart physique offered for the hideous sport of the torture; how his stanch flesh would resist. How long, how long dying he would be!

The terrors of capture by the Cherokees had been by Grant's orders described again and again to the troops to keep the rank and file constant to duty, close in camp, vigilant on out-post, and alert to respond to the call to arms. Never, as Ronald right-eously repeated this grim detail, had he imagined he would ever be in case to remember it with a personal appli-cation. He now protested inwardly that he could die like a soldier. Even from the extremity of physical anguish he had never shrunk. But the hideous prospect of the malice of human fiends wreaked for hours and hours upon every quivering nerve, upon every sensitive fiber, with the wonderful in-genuity for which the Cherokees were famous, made him secretly wince as he crouched there among the friendly Chickasaws, beneath the boughs of the rhododendron splendidly a-bloom in the moonlight, while the rich, pearly glamours of the broken disk sunk down and down the sky, and the dew glim-mered on the full-fleshed leaves, and through them a silver glitter from the Tennessee River hard by struck his eye, and a break in the woods, where the channel curved, showed the contour of a dome of the Great Smoky Mountains limiting the instarred heavens. As he looked out from the covert of the laurel—his flaxen hair visible here and there in rings on his sun-burned forehead, from which his blue bonnet was pushed back; his strongly marked high features, hardly so immobile as was their wont; his belt, his plaid, his claymore, all the details of that ancient martial garb, readjusted with military precision since the fight; his long, rawboned figure, lean and muscular, but nevertheless with a suggestion of the roundness of youth, half reclining, supported on one arm—the Indian gazed at him with questioning intentness.

Suddenly Choolah spoke.

"*Angona*," (friend) he said, with a poignant note of distrust, "you have a thought in your mind."

It was seldom indeed, that Ronald MacDonnell could have been thus accused. He changed color a trifle, although he said, hastily, "Oh, no, my good man, not at all—not at all!"

"*Angona! Angona!*" cried Choolah, in reproach.

Perhaps a definite recognition of this thought in his mind came to MacDonnell with the fear that the Chickasaw, who so easily discerned it, would presently read it. "The fearsome Fox that he is," thought Ronald with an almost superstitious thrill at his heart.

Naturally he could not know how open was that frank face of his, and that the keen discernment of the savage, though perceiving the presence of the withheld thought, was yet inadequate to translate its meaning.

CHOOLAH, THE CHICKASAW

This thought was one which he would in no wise share with Choolah. Mac-Donnell's most coherent mental process was always of a military trend; without a definite effort of discrimination, or even voluntarily reverting to the events of the day, it had suddenly occurred to him that the Cherokee with the essential improvidence of the Indian nature, could not have developed that plan of attack on the provision train, so determined and definitely designed, so difficult to repulse, so repeated, renewed again and again with a desperation of the extremest sacrifice to the end. And small wonder! Its success would have involved the practical destruction of Grant's whole army. Hundreds of miles distant from any sufficient base of supplies, the provision train was the life of the expedition. The beef-herds to be subsequently driven out from the province to Fort Prince George for the use of the army were to be timed with a view to the gradual consumption of the provisions already furnished, and to communicate by messenger to Charlestown, now distant nearly four hundred miles, the disaster of the capture of stores would obviously involve a delay fatal to the troops.

The Indians, however, were a hand-to-mouth nation. Subsisting on the chances of game in their long hunts and marches, enduring in its default incredible rigors of hunger as a matter of course, sustaining life and even strength when in hard luck by roots and fruits and nuts, they could not have realized the value of the provision train to civilized troops who must needs have beef and bacon, flour and tobacco, soap and medicine—or they cannot fight. There was but one explanation—French officers were among the Cherokees and directed these demonstrations. Their presence had been earlier suspected, and this, Ronald thought, was indisputable proof. The strange selection of the ground where in the previous year the Cherokees had massed in force and given battle to Colonel Montgomery's troops had occasioned much surprise, and later the same phenomenon occurred in their engagements with Colonel Grant. It seemed to amount to an exhibition of an intuitive military genius. No great captain of Europe, it was said, could have acted with finer discernment of the opportunities and the dangers, could with greater acumen have avoided and nullified the risks. But Colonel Grant, who was always loath to accord credit to aught but military science, believed the ground was chosen by men who had studied the tactics of the great captains of Europe, and although he had learned to beware of the wily devices of the savage, and to meet his masked fire with skulking scouts and native allies, fighting in their own way, he preserved all the precise tactical methods in which he had been educated, and kept a sharp edge on his expectation for the warlike feints and strategy of the equally trained French officer.

If he could only meet one now, Ronald MacDonnell was thinking. In case it should prove impossible to cross the river and rejoin his command, if he could only surrender to Johnny Crapaud!

To be sure the creature spoke French and ate frogs! More heinous still he was always a Romanist, and diatribes on the wicked sorceries and idolatries of papistry had been hurled through MacDonnell's consciousness from the

Presbyterian pulpit since his earliest recollection. But a soldier, a French officer—surely he would be acquainted with higher methods than the barbarities of the savage; he would be instructed in the humanities, subject to those amenities which in all civilized countries protect a prisoner of war. Surely he would not stand by and see a fellow-soldier—a white man, a Christian, like himself—put to the torture and the stake. And if his authority could not avail for protection—"I'd beg a bullet of him; in charity he could not deny me that!" If the opportunity were but vouchsafed, MacDonnell resolved to appeal to the Frenchman by every sanction that can control a gentleman, by their fellow feeling as soldiers, by the bond of their common religion. He hesitated a moment, realizing a certain hiatus here, a gulf —and then he reconciled all things with a triumphant stroke of potent logic. "They may call it idolatry or Mariolatry, if they want to,—but I never heard anybody deny that the Lord *did* have a mother. And it's a mighty good thing to have!"

This was the thought in his mind—the chance, the hope of surrendering to a French officer.

The stir of the Indians recalled him. The moon was lower in the sky, sinking further and further toward that great purple dome of the many summits of the Great Smoky Mountains. All the glistening lines of light upon the landscape—the glossy foliage, the shining river, the shimmering mists—seemed drawn along as if some fine-spun seine, some glittering enmeshment were being hauled into the boat-shaped moon, still rocking and riding the waves off the headlands that the serrated mountains thrust forth like a coast-line on the seas of the sky. Now and again the voices of creatures of prey—wolves, panthers, wildcats—came shrilly snarling through the summer night from the deep interior of the woods, where they wrangled over the gain that the battle had wrought for them in the slain of horses and men,—of the Cherokee force doubtless; MacDonnell had scarcely a fear that these were of Grant's command, for that officer's care for such protection of his dead as was possible was always immediate and peculiarly marked, and it was his habit to have the bodies sunk with great weights into the rivers to prevent the scalping of them by the Cherokees. Ronald wearied of the melancholy hours, the long, long night, although light would have but added dangers of discovery. It was the lagging time he would hasten, would fain stride into the future and security, so did the suspense wear on his nerves. It told heavily even on the Indian, and Ronald felt a certain sympathy when Choolah's half-suppressed voice greeted the scout, creeping into the grotto once more, with the wistful inquiry, "*Onna He-tak?*" (Is it day?)

But the news that the *Etissu* brought was not indeed concerned with the hour. In his opinion, they would all soon have little enough to do with time. His intelligence was in truth alarming. While the Cherokees patrolling the river had gradually withdrawn to the interior of the forest and disappeared, those at the ford above were suspiciously astir. They had received evidently some intimation of the presence here of the lurking Chickasaws, and were on the watch. To seek to flee would precipitate an instant attack; to escape hence would be merely to fall into the hands of the marauders in the forest beyond; to plunge into the Tennessee River would furnish a floating target for the unerring marksmen. Yet the crisis was immediate.

Choolah suddenly raised the hand of authority.

Ronald MacDonnell had seen much service, and had traveled far out of the beaten paths of life. He was born a gentleman of good means and of long descent—for if the MacDonnells were to be believed, Adam was hardly a patch upon the antiquity of the great Clan-Colla. He had already made an excellent record in his profession. It seemed to him the veriest reversal of all the probabilities that he should now be called upon to take his orders from Choolah the Fox, the savage Chickasaw. Yet he felt no immediate vocation for the command, had it been within his reach. With all his military talent and training he could devise no other resource than to withstand the attack of the larger party with half their number; to swim the river, and drown there with a musketball in his brain; to flee into the woods to certain capture. He watched, therefore, with intensest curiosity the movements of the men under Choolah's direction. The moon was now very low, the light golden, dully burnished, far-striking, with a long shadow. First one, then another of the Chickasaws showed themselves openly upon the bank of the river in a clear space high above the current of the water. Choolah beckoned to the Scotchman, and MacDonnell alertly sprang to his feet and joined the wily tactician without a question, aware that he was assisting to baffle the terrible enemy. His bonnet, his fluttering plaid, his swinging claymore, his great muscular height and long stride, all defined in the moonlight against the soft sky and the mountains beyond, were enough to acquaint the watching Cherokees with the welcome fact that here was not only an enemy but a white man of the Highland battalion, the friends of the Chickasaw. The artful Chickasaws swiftly and confusedly came and went from the densities of the laurel. Impossible it would have been for the Cherokees to judge definitely of their numbers, so quickly did they appear and disappear and succeed one another. Thus cleverly the attack was postponed.

Ronald MacDonnell gave full credit to the strategy of Choolah. For it would now seem—it needs must—that their little party no longer feared the enemies in the quiet woods! They must have presumed the Cherokees all gone! The Chickasaws were building a fire since the moon was sinking.

Probably they felt they could not lie down to sleep without its protection and wolves very near in the woods. Listen to that shrill, blood-curdling cry! They were surely disposing themselves to rest! Already as the blaze began to leap up and show in the water of the river below like a great red jewel, with the deep crystalline lusters of a many-faceted ruby, figures might be seen by the flare of the mounting flames, recumbent on the ground, wrapped in blankets; here and there was tartan, an end of the plaid thrown over the face as the Highlanders always slept; here and there a hunting-shirt and leggings were plainly visible—all lying like the spokes of a wheel around the central point of the fire.

"It is only the Muscogees who sleep in line," Choolah explained to Mac-Donnell, who had criticised the disposition.

CHOOLAH, THE CHICKASAW

The crafty Cherokees, stealthily approaching ever nearer and nearer, had not seen in the first feeble glimmers of the flames the figures of the seven men crawling gingerly back to the grotto in the covert of the laurel, leaving around the fire merely billets of wood arrayed in the blankets and stolen gear which the Owl had brought off from the battle-field.

"But I am always in the wrong," plained Oop-pa, sarcastically. "What would you and the big tartan-man have to dress those warriors in if I had not stayed for my goods?"

MacDonnell had urged his scruples. This was hardly according to the rules of war. "But if the Cherokees fire on sleeping men," he argued—

"*Angona*," the wily Chickasaw assured him, suavely, "they are disarmed. We can rush out and overpower them before they can load."

"They ought to be able to fire three times to the minute," thought Mac-Donnell, who was a good drill.

But the Cherokees were not held to the rigorous manual of arms, and did not attain to that degree of dexterity considered excellent efficiency in that day although a breech-loading musket invented by Colonel Patrick Ferguson, who met his death at King's Mountain, was capable of being fired seven times a minute, and was used not many years after these events, with destructive effect, by his own command at the battle of the Brandywine, in 1777.

MacDonnell, lying prone on the ground in the laurel, his face barely lifted, saw the last segment of the moon slip down behind the great mountain, the following mists glister in the after-glow and fade, a soft, dull shadow drop upon the landscape then

CHOOLAH, THE CHICKASAW

sink to darkness, and in the blaze of the fire a quivering feather-crested head protrude above the river-bank. There were other crafty approaches—here, there, the woods seemed alive! Suddenly an alien flare of light, a series of funnel-shaped evanescent darts, the simultaneous crack of a volley, and a dozen swift figures dashed to the scalping of their victims by the fire—to lay hold on the logs in the likeness of sleeping men, to break a knife in the hard fibers of one that seemed to stir, to cry aloud, inarticulate, wild, frenzied in rage, in amaze, in grief, to find themselves at the mercy of the Chickasaws darting out from the laurel!

There was a tumultuous rush, then a frantic, futile attempt to reload; two or three of the prisoners wielding knives with undue effect were shot down, and Choolah, triumphant, majestic in victory, stately, erect, his crown of tall white swan's feathers, his glittering fringes of roanoke, the red and blue of his glossy war-paint, all revealed by the flaring fire, waved his hand to his "*Angona*" to call upon him to admire his prowess in battle.

The next moment his attention was caught by a sudden swift alarm in the face of one of the Cherokees, a far-away glance that the wily Choolah followed with his quick eye. Something had happened at the camp the Cherokees had abandoned—was there still movement there?

It was some one who had been away, returning, startled to see the bivouac fire sunken to an ember,—for the Cherokees had let it die out to further the advantages of the attack,—then evidently reassured to note the flare a little further down the stream, as if the camp had been shifted for some reason.

CHOOLAH, THE CHICKASAW

Choolah drew his primed and loaded pistol. No Cherokee, however, would have dared to venture a warning sign. And Ronald MacDonnell, with what feelings he could hardly analyze, could never describe, saw leaping along the jagged bank of the river toward them a white man, young, active, wearing a gayly-fringed hunting-shirt and leggings of buckskin, but a military hat and the gorget of a French officer. He was among them before he saw his mistake—his fatal mistake! The delighted shrieks of the Chickasaws overpowered every sense, filling the woods with their fierce shrill joy and seeming to strike against the very sky, "*French! hottuk ook-proo-se!*" (The accursed people!)

All thought of caution, all fears of wandering Cherokees were lost in the supreme ecstasy of their triumph—the capture of one of the detested French, that the tribe had hated with an inconceivable and savage rancor for generations.

"*Shukapa! Shukapa!*" (Swine-eater!) they exclaimed in disgust and derision, for the aversion of the Indians to pork was equaled only by that of the Jews, and this was an extreme expression of contempt.

The captive was handled rudely enough in the process of disarming him, which the Owl and Choolah accomplished, while his Cherokees stood at the muzzles of the firelocks of the others. There was blood on his face and hands as he turned a glance on the Scotchman. He uttered a few eager words in French, unintelligible to MacDonnell save the civil preface, "*Pardon, Monsieur, mais puis-je vous demander—*"

The rest of the sentence was lost in the fierce derisive shrieks of the Chickasaws recognizing the inflections of the detested language, *"Seente soolish! Seente soolish!"* (snake's tongue!) they vociferated.

But had the conclusion of the request been audible it would have been incomprehensible to Ronald MacDonnell.

The impassive Highlander silently shook his head, and a certain fixity of despair settled on the face of the French officer. It was a young face— he seemed not more than twenty-five, MacDonnell thought. It was narrow, delicately molded, with very bright eyes, that had a sort of youthful daring in them—adventurous looking eyes. They were gray, with long black lashes and strongly defined eyebrows. His complexion was of a clear healthy pallor, his hair dark but a trifle rough, and braided in the usual queue. So often did Ronald

MacDonnell have to describe this man, both on paper and off, that every detail of his appearance grew very familiar to him. The stranger's lips were red and full, and the upper one was short and curving; he did not laugh or smile, of course, but he showed narrow white teeth, for now and again he gasped as if for breath, and more than once that sensitive upper lip quivered. Not that Ronald MacDonnell ever gave the portraiture in this simple wise, for his descriptions were long and involved, minute and yet vague, and proved the despair of all interested in fixing the identity of the man; but gleaning from his accounts this is the way the stranger must have appeared to the young Scotchman. His figure was tall and lightly built, promising more activity than muscular force, and while one hand was held on the buckle of his belt, the left went continually to the hilt of a sword, *which he did not wear*, but the habit was betrayed by this gesture. There was nothing about him to intimate his rank, beyond the gorget, and on this point Ronald MacDonnell could never give any satisfaction.

The Indian is seldom immoderate in laughter, but Choolah could not restrain his wicked mirth to discover that the two officers could not speak to each other. And yet the pale-faces were so often amazed that the Cherokees and the Chickasaws and the Creeks had not the same language, as if a variety of tongues were thrown away on the poor Indian, who might well be expected to put up with one speech! For only the Chickasaw and Choctaw dialects were inter-comprehensible, both tribes being descended, it is said, from the ancient Chickemicaws, and in fact much of the variation in their speech was but a matter of intonation. The tears of mirth stood in Choolah's eyes. He held his hand to his side—he could scarcely calm himself, even when he discerned a special utility in this lack of a medium of communication, for the enterprising scout came back once more to say that there were some Chickasaws lower down on the river, where the ford was better. Choolah received this assurance with most uncommon demonstrations of pleasure, evidently desiring their assistance in guarding the prisoners to Grant's camp, being ambitious of securing the commander's commendation and intending to afford ocular proof of his exploit by exhibiting the number of his captives. But MacDonnell detected a high note of elation in Choolah's voice which no mere pride could evoke, and he recognized a danger signal. He instantly bethought himself of the fate at the hands of the

CHOOLAH, THE CHICKASAW

Chickasaws, more than a score of years befoṙe, of the gallant D'Artaguette, the younger, and his brave lieutenant Vincennes, burned at the stake by slow fires, after their unhappy defeat at the fortified town, *Ash-wick-boo-ma* (Red Grass), the noble Jesuit, Sénat, sharing their death, although he might have escaped, remaining to comfort their last moments with his ghostly counsels.

MacDonnell listened as warily to the talk as he might, and although Choolah said no more than was eminently natural in planning to turn over his prisoners to these Chickasaws by reason of their superior numbers, MacDonnell's alert sense detected the same vibration when he expressed his decision to leave the *Etissu* and the Highland officer to guard the Frenchman till his return.

"Then we will together cross the Tennessee river here," he said.

MacDonnell yawned widely as he nodded his head, his hand over his stretched mouth and shielding his face. He would not trust its expression to the discerning Choolah, for he had again that infrequent guest, "a thought in his mind."

In truth, Choolah had no intention to take the Frenchman to Grant's camp. The praise he would receive as a reward was a petty consideration indeed as compared with the delights of torturing and burning so rare, so choice a victim as a French officer. To be sure his excuse must be good and devised betimes, for Colonel Grant was squeamish and queer, objecting to the scalping and burning of prisoners, and seemed indeed at times of a weak stomach in regard to such details. And that came about naturally enough. He did not fast, as behooves a war-captain. He ate too much on the war-path. He had two cooks! He had also a man to dress his hair, and another to groom his horse. Naturally his heart had softened, and he was averse to the stern pleasures of recompensing an enemy with the anguish of the stake. This Choolah intended to enjoy, summoning the Chickasaws at the ford below to the scene of his triumph. Besides it requires a number of able-bodied assistants to properly roast in wet weather a vigorous and protesting captive. The Scotchman should suspect naught until his return. True, he might not object, for were not the French as ever the inveterate enemies of the English? But if he should it could avail naught against the will of a round dozen or more of Chicka-saws. Besides, was not the prisoner of the detested nation of the French

—*Nana-Ubat?* (Nothings and brothers to nothing.) Nevertheless, it was well they could not speak to each other and possibly canvass fears and offer persuasions. He could spare only one man, the scout, to aid in the watch, but he felt quite assured. Ronald MacDonnell was always notoriously vigilant and exacting, and was held in great fear by guards and outposts and sentinels, for often his rounds were attended by casualties in the way of reprimand, and arrests, and guard-tent sojourns and discipline. Choolah felt quite safe as he set off at a brisk pace with his squad of four Chickasaws, driving the disarmed Cherokees, silent and sullen, before him.

They were hardly out of sight when MacDonnell, kicking the enveloping blanket out of the way, sat down on one of the logs by the fire and spread his big bony hands out to the blaze.

CHOOLAH, THE CHICKASAW

It was growing chill; the June night was wearing on toward the dawn; it was that hour of reduced vitality when hope seems of least value, and the blood runs low, and conscience grows keen, and the future and the past bear heavily alike on the present. The prisoner was shivering slightly. He glanced expectantly at the Scotchman's impassive countenance. No man knew better than Ronald MacDonnell the churlishness of a lack of consideration of the comfort of others in small matters. No man could offer little attentions more genially. They comported essentially with his evident breeding, and his rank in the army; once more the prisoner looked expectantly at him, and then, wounded, like a Frenchman, as for a host's lack of consideration, he sat down on a log uninvited, casting but one absent glance, from which curiosity seemed expunged, at the effigies which explained how the Cherokees came to their fate. It mattered little now, his emotional, sensitive face said. Naught mattered! Naught! Naught!

In the sudden nervous shock his vitality was at its lowest ebb. He could not spread his hands to the blaze, for his arms had been pinioned cruelly tight. He shivered again, for the fire was low. MacDonnell noticed it, but he did not stir; perhaps he thought Johnny Crapaud would soon find the fire hot enough. The scout himself mended it, as he sat tailorwise on the ground between the other two men. Now and again the *Etissu* gazed at MacDonnell's impassive, rather lowering countenance, with a certain awe; if he had expected the officer to show the squeamishness which Colonel Grant developed in such matters, or any pity, he was mistaken; then he looked with curiosity at the Frenchman. The prisoner's lips were vaguely moving, and Ronald MacDonnell caught a suggestion of the sound—half-whispered words, not French, or he would not have understood; Latin!—paters and aves! As he had expected — frogs, papistry, French, and fool!

"What's that?" the Highland officer said, so suddenly that the scout started in affright.

"Nothing," said the Indian; "the wind, perhaps."

"Sticks cracking in the laurel—a bear, perhaps," suggested MacDonnell, taking up a loaded musket and laying it across his knee. Then "Only a bear," he repeated reassuringly.

"Choolah ought to leave more men here," said the *Etissu*.

"It's nothing!" declared MacDonnell, rising and looking warily about. "Perhaps Choolah on his way back."

The scout was true to his vagrant tendencies, or perhaps because of those tendencies he felt himself safer in the dense, impenetrable jungle, crawling along flat like a lizard or a snake, than seated perched up here on a bluff by a flaring camp-fire with only two other men, a mark for "Brown Bess"—the Cherokees were all armed with British muskets, although they were in revolt, and perhaps it was one reason why they were in revolt—for many a yard up and down the Tennessee River. "I go see," he suggested.

"No, no," said MacDonnell, "only a bear."

"I come back soon," declared the *Etissu*, half crouching and gazing about, "soon, soon. *Alooska, Ko-e-u-que-ho.*" (I do not lie, I do not indeed.)

MacDonnell lifted his head and gazed about with a frowning mien of reluctance "*Maia cha!*" (Go along) he said at last. Then called out, "Come back *soon*," as his attention returned to the priming and loading of a pistol which he had in progress. "Soon! remember!"

The scout was off like a rabbit. For a moment or two MacDonnell did not lift his eyes, while they heard him crashing through the thicket. Then as he looked up he met the dull despair in the face of the bound and helpless Frenchman. It mattered little to him who came, who went. He gasped suddenly in amazement. The Highland officer was gazing at him with a genial, boyish smile, reassuring, almost tender.

"Run, now, run for your life!" he said, leaning forward, and with a pass or two of a knife he severed the prisoner's bonds.

In the revulsion of feeling the man

seemed scarcely able to rise to his feet. There were tears in his eyes; his face quivered as he looked at his deliverer.

"Danger—big fire—burn," said the astute MacDonnell, as if the English words thus detached were more comprehensible to the French limitations. Perhaps his gestures aided their effect, and as he held out his hand in his whole-souled, genial way, the Frenchman grasped it in a hard grip of fervent gratitude and started off swiftly. The next moment the young officer turned back, caught the British soldier in his arms, and to MacDonnell's everlasting consternation kissed him in the foreign fashion, first on one cheek and then on the other.

Ronald MacDonnell's mess often preyed upon the disclosures which his open, ingenuous nature afforded them. But his simplicity stopped far short of revealing to them this Gallic demonstration of gratitude—so exquisitely ludicrous it seemed to his unemotional methods and mind. They were debarred the pleasure of racking him on this circumstance. They never knew it. He disclosed it only years afterward, and then by accident, to a member of his own family.

The whole affair seemed to the mess serious enough. For the Chickasaws, baffled and furious, had threatened his life on their return, reinforced by a dozen excited, elated, expectant tribesmen, laden with light wood and a chain, to find their prisoner gone. But after the first wild outburst of rage and despair Choolah, although evidently strongly tempted to force the Highlander to the fate from which he had rescued the French officer, resolved to preserve the integrity of his nation's pledge of amity with the British, and restrained his men from offering injury. This was rendered the more acceptable to him, as with his alert craft he perceived a keen retribution for Ronald MacDonnell in the displeasure of his commanding officer, for the Chickasaws well understood the discipline of the army, which they chose to disregard. To better enlist the prejudice of Colonel Grant, Choolah was preparing himself to distort the facts. He upbraided Ronald MacDonnell with causelessly liberating a prisoner, a Frenchman and an officer, taken by the wily exploit of another. As to the dry wood, he said, the Chickasaws had merely brought some drift, long stranded in a cave by the waterside, to replenish the fire, kindled with how great difficulty in the soaking condition of the forests the Lieutenant well knew.

"Hout!—just now when we are about to cross the river?" cried Ronald, unmasking the subterfuge. "And for what then that stout chain?"

The chain, Choolah protested, was but part of the equipment of one of the pack animals that had broken away and had been plundered by the Cherokees. Did the Lieutenant Plaidman think he wanted to chain the prisoner to the stake to burn? He had had no dream of such a thing! It was not the custom of the Chickasaws to waste so much time on a prisoner. It was sufficient to cut him up in quarters; that usually killed him dead,—quite dead enough! But if the Lieutenant had had a chain, since he knew so well the use of one, doubtless he himself would have joyed to burn the prisoner, provided it had been his own exploit that had taken him,—for did not the Carolinians of the provincial regiment say that when the Tartan men were at home they were as wild and as uncivilized as the wildest Cherokee savage!

"*Holauba! Holauba! Feenah!*" (It is a lie. It is a lie, undoubtedly), cried the phlegmatic MacDonnell, excited to a frenzy. He spoke in the Chickasaw language, that the insult might be understood as offered with full intention.

But Choolah did not thus receive it. In the simplicity of savage life lies are admittedly the natural incidents of conversation. He addressed himself anew to argument. At home the Tartan men lived in mountains,—just like the Cherokees,—and no wonder they were undismayed by the war whoops—they had heard the like before! Savages themselves! They had a language, too, that the Carolinians could not speak; he himself had heard it among the Highlanders of Grant's camp—doubtless it was the

Cherokee tongue, for they were mere Cherokees!

"Holauba! Holauba! Feenah!" No denial could be more definite than the tone and the words embodied.

The wily Choolah, maliciously delighted with his power to pierce the heart of the proud Scotchman thus, turned the knife anew. Did not the provincials declare that the Highlanders at home were always beaten in war, as they would be here but for the help of the Carolinians?

"Holauba! Holauba! Feenah!" protested Ronald resolutely, thinking of Preston Pans and Falkirk.

For the usual emulous bickering between regulars and provincials, which seems concomitant with every war, had appeared in full force in this expedition, the provincials afterward claiming that but for them and their Indian allies no remnant of the British force would have returned alive; and the regulars declaring that the Carolinians knew nothing, and could learn nothing of discipline and method in warfare, laying great stress on the fact that this was the second campaign to which the British soldiers had been summoned for the protection of the province, which could not without them defend itself against the Cherokees, and assuming the entire credit of the subjugation of that warlike tribe that had for nearly a century past desolated at intervals the Carolina borders.

Although it had been Choolah's hope that, by means of provoking against the Lieutenant the displeasure of his superior officer, he might revenge himself upon MacDonnell, for snatching from the Chickasaws the peculiar racial delight of torturing the French prisoner, the Indians had no anticipation of the gravity of the crisis when they came to the camp with the details of the occurrence, which, to Colonel Grant's annoyance, tallied with MacDonnell's own report of himself.

For there was a question in Colonel Grant's mind whether the prisoner were not the redoubtable Louis Latinac, who had been so incredibly efficient in the French interest in this region, and who had done more to excite the enmity of the Cherokees against their quondam allies, the British, and harass his Majesty's troops than a regiment of other men could accomplish. When Grant tended to this opinion, a court-martial seemed impending over the head of the young officer.

"What was your reason for this extraordinary course?" Colonel Grant asked.

And Ronald MacDonnell answered

that he had granted to his prisoner exactly what he had intended to demand of his captor had the situation been reversed—to adjure him by their fellow feeling as soldiers, by the customs of civilized warfare, by the bond of a common religion, to save him from torture by savages.

"Can a gentleman give less than he would ask?" he demanded.

And when Colonel Grant would urge that he should have trusted to his authority to protect the prisoner, Ronald would meet the argument with the counter-argument that the Indians respected no authority, and in cases of fire it would not do to take chances.

"Why did you not at least exact a parole?"

"Lord, sir, we couldn't talk at all!" said Ronald, conclusively. "In common humanity, I was obliged to release him or shoot him, and I could not shoot an unarmed prisoner to save my life—not if I were to be shot for it myself.''

Lieutenant - Colonel Grant's heart was well known to be soft in spots. He has put it upon record in the previous campaign against the Cherokees that he could not help pitying them a little in the destruction of their homes, —it is said, however, that after this later expedition his name was incorporated in the Cherokee language as a synonym of devastation and a cry of warning. He was overcome by the considerations urged upon him by the Lieutenant until once more the possibility loomed upon the horizon that it was Louis Latinac who had escaped him, when he would feel that nothing but Ronald MacDonnell's best heart's blood could atone for the release. To set this much vexed question at rest the young officer was repeatedly required to describe the personal appearance of the stranger, and thus it was that poor Ronald's verbal limitations were brought so conspicuously forward. "A fine man," he would say one day, and in giving the details of that sensitive emotional countenance which had so engaged his interest that momentous night — its force, its suggestiveness, its bright, alert young eyes, would intimate that he had indeed held the motive power of the Cherokee war in his hand, and had heedlessly loosed it as a child might release a butterfly. The next day "a braw callant" was about the sum of his conclusions, and Colonel Grant would be certain that the incident represented no greater matter than the escape of a brisk subaltern, like Ronald himself. In the course of Colonel Grant's anxious vacillations of opinion, the young Highlander was given to understand that he would be instantly placed under arrest, but for the fact that every officer of experience was urgently needed. And indeed Colonel Grant presently had his hands quite full, fighting a furious battle only the ensuing day with the entire Cherokee nation.

The Indians attacked his outposts at eight o'clock in the morning, and with their full strength engaged the main body, fighting in their individual, skulking, masked manner, but with fierce persistency for three hours; then the heat of the conflict began to gradually wane, although they did not finally draw off till two o'clock in the afternoon. It was the last struggle of the Cherokee war. Helpless or desperate, the Indians watched without so much as a shot from ambush the desolation of their country. For thirty days Colonel Grant's forces remained among the fastnesses of the Great Smoky Mountains, devastating those beautiful valleys, burning "the astonishing magazines of corn," and the towns, which Grant states, were so "agreeably situated, the houses neatly built." Often the troops were constrained to march under the beetling heights of those stupendous ranges, whence one might imagine a sharp musketry fire would have destroyed the dense columns, almost to the last man. Perhaps the inability of the French to furnish the Cherokees with the requisite ammunition for this campaign may explain the abandonment of a region so calculated for effective defense.

Aside from the losses in slain and wounded in the engagement, the expeditionary force suffered much, for the hardships of the campaign were extreme. Having extended the frontier westward by seventy miles, and withdrawing slowly, in view of the gradual exhaustion of his supplies, Colonel Grant found the feet of his infantry so mangled by the long and continuous marches in the rugged country west of the Great Smoky Mountains that he was forced to go into permanent camp on returning to Fort Prince George, to permit the rest and recovery of the soldiers, who in fact could march no further, as well as to await some action on the part of the Cherokee rulers looking to the conclusion of a peace.

A delegation of chiefs presently sought audience of him here and agreed to all the stipulations of the treaty formulated in behalf of the province except one, viz., that four Cherokees should be delivered up to be put to death in the presence of Colonel Grant's army, or that four green scalps should be brought to him within the space of twelve nights. With this article the chiefs declared they had neither the will nor the power to comply,—and very queerly indeed, it reads at this late day!

Colonel Grant, perhaps willing to elude the enforcement of so unpleasant a requisition, conceived that it lay within his duty to forward the delegation, under escort, to Charlestown to seek to induce Governor Bull to mitigate its rigor.

It was in this connection that he alluded again to the release of the prisoner, captured in the exploit of Choolah, the Chickasaw, although in conversation with his officers he seemed to Ronald MacDonnell to be speaking only of the impracticable stipulation of the treaty, and his certainty that compliance would not be required of the Cherokees by the Governor—and in fact the terms finally signed at Charlestown, on the 10th of December of that year, were thus moderated, leaving the compact practically the same as in the previous treaty of 1759.

"I could agree to no such stipulation if the case were mine," Colonel Grant declared, "that four of my soldiers, as a mere matter of intimidation, should be surrendered to be executed in the presence of the enemy! Certainly, as a gentleman and a soldier, a man cannot require of an enemy more than he himself would be justified in yielding if the circumstances were reversed, or grant to an enemy less favor than he himself could rightfully ask at his hands."

Ronald MacDonnell had forgotten his own expression of this sentiment. It appealed freshly to him, and he thought it decidedly fine. He did not recognize a flag of truce except as a veritable visible white rag, and from time to time he experienced much surprise that Colonel Grant did not order him under arrest as a preliminary to a court martial.